Praise for *Greenwich* . . .

"A solid piece of fiction . . . a well-plotted tale of murder, intrigue, integrity and suspense." —*Press Journal* (Vero Beach, FL)

"Fast has lost none of his storytelling skills . . . an exhilaratingly rapid read that deals with some far from negligible ideas."
—*Publishers Weekly*

"Over the years, Fast, who first grabbed us with the freshness of *Freedom Road*, *Citizen Tom Paine*, and later *Spartacus*, has continued as a civil libertarian, mixing in the occasional novels of sheer macaronic entertainment (throw in anything) such as his latest." —*Kirkus Reviews*

"Fast's faithful readers anticipate each new novel, and *Greenwich* meets all expectations. Recommended for all fiction collections."
—*Library Journal*

"In a droll shift of perspective, Fast gives the reader intermittent glimpses of the main figures." —*BookPage*

Praise for *Redemption* . . .

"Provocative." —*Entertainment Weekly*

"Eminently readable." —*Publishers Weekly*

"A shuddering, edge-of-your-seat climax."
—*Knoxville News-Sentinel*

"His dialogue is a joy to read . . . reminiscent of the crisp style of Raymond Chandler." —*The Denver Post*

"A Wall Street businessman is found shot in the back of the head at his desk, where he'd just written a check to 'Cash' for $100,000 but hadn't had a chance to sign it. And a woman stands on a bridge, contemplating tossing herself over the rail, when a seventy-eight-year-old retired Columbia law professor stops her. You'd think this was a thriller with a beginning like that. But it's not. It's a much more subtle, psychological drama, told in a thoughtful and riveting manner. . . . The book asks the question, Can one person ever truly know another?" —*Pittsburgh Post-Gazette*

continued on the next page . . .

ALSO BY HOWARD FAST

GREENWICH

HOWARD FAST

JOVE BOOKS, NEW YORK

This is a work of fiction. Names, characters, places, and incidents either are the product of the author's imagination or are used fictitiously, and any resemblance to actual persons, living or dead, business establishments, events, or locales is entirely coincidental.

GREENWICH

A Jove Book / published by arrangement with
Harcourt, Inc.

PRINTING HISTORY
Harcourt, Inc. hardcover edition / May 2000
Jove edition / June 2002

Visit our website at
www.penguinputnam.com

ISBN: 0-515-13346-9

A JOVE BOOK®
Jove Books are published by The Berkley Publishing Group,
a division of Penguin Putnam Inc.,
375 Hudson Street, New York, New York 10014.
JOVE and the "J" design
are trademarks belonging to Penguin Putnam Inc.

PRINTED IN THE UNITED STATES OF AMERICA

10 9 8 7 6 5 4 3 2 1

For Mimi O'Connor Fast

PART ONE   *Friday*

One

At seven o'clock in the morning, the June sun, fighting its way through the curtains of Muffy's bedroom, awakened her, as it did every other summer morning. She had long resolved that she would replace the curtains with impenetrable drapes, but as with so many other resolutions, it remained undone. How she envied women who could curl up under the covers until eleven and even noon! The dark mornings of winter made no difference. At 7:00 A.M. she was awake, and if she tried to remain in bed, she paid the price of aching limbs.

Mornings were the worst; each morning she faced a long and boring day. Unlike so many of her female friends, she played neither tennis nor golf. She disliked both, after having made a feeble try at both. When her children were young, they were at least a distraction if not entirely a blessing. The long hours she had spent at hockey and soccer games had bored her to tears. Her husband—her second marriage—was an investment banker employed by a Swiss bank, and if he was not in Brazil or Taiwan, he was in Switzerland. Her three children came by her first husband, and they were all in college now, spending their summers with her first husband in San Franciso.

In her thoughts, her husband, Martin—or Matt as everyone called him—was a disaster, visited upon her and to be endured. She had run out of affairs, except for an occasional assignation with a neighbor, one Richard Castle, who also lived in the Back Country of Greenwich, an area north of the Merritt Parkway inhabited by the great houses of Greenwich. She could easily get two million for her own house in today's market and Muffy dreamed about selling it and moving to the East Side of New York, but Matt would have no part of that, even though one of her friends—one of a number who were real-estate agents—had assured her that in another few months the price would go to three million.

Most of her neighbors were involved in charity work of one sort or another, but with Matt's constant anger at the taxes he paid, she felt that the government could afford to take care of charity and that to work for nothing was meaningless. Thus, this beautiful Friday morning offered nothing better than boredom. She could take in a midday movie, but while she did this occasionally, she always confronted the fear that one of her acquaintances might see her sitting alone, a confession of how lonely she was. She might drive into New York, but there were no matinees she desired to see on Friday, and her morning languor resisted the thought of a long drive through traffic.

Another empty hour drifted by when her thoughts were interrupted by the telephone. She didn't rush to pick it up, thinking that it was probably Matt calling from one of the godforsaken places he did his business in. But it was not Matt, but Sally Castle, who lived on the next road.

"I know I shouldn't be calling you now," Sally said apologetically, "but I know you rise early, don't you?"

"I was awake," Muffy said evenly, waiting to sharpen or lighten her tone until she found out what this was all about.

"I mean," Sally went on, still apologetic, "that it's terrible to call you on the same day and invite you to a dinner party, but I know Matt's away on business . . ." Sally's voice trailed off. Sally knew she should have mentioned that she was sure Muffy had another offer or date for this evening, but she didn't know exactly how to put it.

"Did you say a dinner party?" Muffy asked.

"Yes. And I hired Abel Hunt to cook. You know what a wonderful cook he is."

Of course, Muffy thought. You're a dumb bitch who can't boil an egg properly, from what Richard says; but she said, "Abel Hunt! How delightful! Will Richard be there?"

"Oh, yes."

"I do have another date," Muffy said regretfully.

"Oh, no. I'm so sorry."

"But I'm sure I can get out of it—you know, a sick headache and all that sort of thing. What time?"

"I'm so glad, Muffy. Will seven-thirty be all right?"

"Perfect."

Muffy put down the telephone and said aloud, "Well, what do you know! How dumb can a dumb broad be?"

She stripped off her nightgown and stood naked in front of her full-length mirror. Not too bad, she thought. Her breast augmentation of two years past had given her the profile of a twenty-year-old. She was a tall woman, and with a tummy tuck and a lift or two, her forty-five years did not show. She was a good-looking woman, and she decided she would spend the afternoon getting her hair roots done. She was not as pretty as Sally Castle, who was five years younger, but neither had she been bought and paid for.

Sister Patricia Brody was plump. A heartless person might well refer to her as being fat. But most people who met her for the first time were taken by her round, pretty face and her open smile. Sister Brody was a missionary nun who had been transferred from Central America to Greenwich, Connecticut, and St. Matthew's Parish some three months before, as it was put to Monsignor Donovan, for rest and recuperation—both of which she badly needed. Since then, she had gained twelve pounds and prayed daily for forgiveness for dereliction of duty and enjoyment of the peace in a quiet and lovely Connecticut town.

When she spoke of her guilt to her new boss, Father Donovan, a tall, gaunt, and fleshless man, he said sternly, "Guilt, my dear Sister, for something you have not done is totally wasteful. Even though there are no bullet holes in our church and you can walk down the street with no danger of being chopped in two with a machete, there is still useful work to be done. So I suggest that you stop asking for forgiveness, because there is nothing to forgive."

She recalled that conversation today, on this Friday morning in June, as she tapped on Monsignor Donovan's office door. His door was never locked, but she had never felt privileged to open a door, any door, and walk in.

"Come in, please," the priest said.

She entered the small, simple room, furnished with a desk, a filing cabinet, and some chairs.

"Sit down, please, Sister."

She seated herself and folded her hands in her lap, trying to recall whatever she might have done wrong.

"I need a favor from you."

"Of course," she said with relief.

"I have an invitation to dinner tonight, a rather unusual invitation. I would like you to accompany me."

Sister Brody nodded.

"I trust you are in good health and enjoying your work here?"

"Very good health. I've gained—" She was going to add the burden of the dismal twelve pounds, but she thought better of it.

"People love you. I think that's the highest mark of achievement."

"Thank you, Father."

"I'll be driving there—it's in what they call the Back Country here in Greenwich. So if you meet me at the front entrance at, say, six forty-five, we'll be there at the proper time, more or less. We can talk about the problem while we drive. It concerns a young woman, and I don't feel I'm equipped to deal with it."

It was not that Sister Brody was in awe of the monsignor, whom she had come to know rather well, but the situation here was very new to her. Since she saw Father Donovan every day, she considered it somewhat odd that he should ask about her health. She knew that she had a sharp tongue, so his remark about people loving her was obviously meant to say something about the coming evening.

"I'll try to be very diplomatic, whatever it is," the nun said.

"Pat, that is not what I meant."

She smiled, and the monsignor shook his head.

"What shall I wear?" she asked.

"Good heavens, I don't know. What you're wearing now. You look fine just as you are."

"I'll find something."

"Six forty-five, at the church entrance."

It had finally stopped raining. Between five and seven inches of rain had fallen in the past six days, depending on which corner of Fairfield County did the measuring; and Herb Greene, sitting in his favorite porch chair—by tacit agreement with his wife, Mary, he did not smoke cigars indoors—lit his first cigar of the day and prepared to assault the *New York Times* crossword puzzle.

Mary came out to the old-fashioned porch, sniffed, grimaced, and asked why he hadn't saved the cigar for after dinner.

"We agreed on two a day. This is my first. I suggest you look at the cane. You can almost watch it grow. It must grow inches every day. I meant to put a stick in and measure it, but I never got around to that. It's odd that each year there are more and more things that I never get around to. Thank God it's stopped raining. If this were a northeaster, every ten-million-dollar home on the shore would be awash. What's a seven-letter word for *complaisant*?"

Mary, listening patiently and without irritation, did not bother to point out that he was a professor of linguistics; instead she said shortly, "Willing."

"I tried that. It doesn't work."

Mary Greene was a tall, handsome woman. In Herb's mind, it was handsome rather than good-looking or beautiful. Her features were strong and sharp; her mouth wide, full; her hair cropped close; her eyes deep set and brown. She had just turned fifty, her hair beginning to streak gray. She wore jeans and a cotton shirt.

"I'm going to get dressed," she said. "It's almost six. Do you intend to arrive in blue jeans?"

"Arrive? Arrive where?"

"At the Castles'—for dinner. Herb, what on earth are you doing? You don't have memory lapses."

"I thought we discussed that," he protested. "I said I did not want to socialize with the Castles or have dinner with another damned investment banker or hear anything about bond spreads or IPOs or the price of sowbellies—"

"Yes, you said all that. And I said we had to go because I accepted this invitation two weeks ago; and out of love and sympathy for your wife and for the enormous mortgage on the town's new library, you retreated."

"I retreated. I always do, because I'm a mild and unaggressive man—"

"What! Please say that again." She shook her head. "No, don't say that again."

"Now you're pissed off."

Herbert Greene sighed and placed his cigar carefully in

the ashtray next to the chair. "This is still number one, the first cigar today. If I light it when we come home, remember that. Anyway, Castle's an anti-Semite."

"Oh, Herb, come on. Sally says she invited Harold Sellig, the writer. He's dying to meet you."

"Two of us. So it's Jew night."

"Yes, and since I'm going to be there, that makes it Catholic night. You don't change."

"What would you like me to change into?"

"I picked up both of your lightweight flannels at the cleaners today. You have a choice."

"Bless you." He rose and kissed her. She was five nine. He was six feet and two inches, a skinny, gangly man, with thinning carrot hair and a reddish beard turning white.

"I'll shower," he said. It was the ultimate surrender, and after he had gone into the house, Mary stood on the porch for a few minutes, looking at the smoking cigar he had left behind and thinking that she'd give a great deal for a cigarette at this moment. Well, she had not smoked for seven years, and she was never going to go through kicking the habit again. When he surrendered an argument, she always felt compassion for him. This month, their marriage would be thirty years old; and all things considered, she decided, it had been good as marriages go. She still loved him, or perhaps she nurtured him; and what was the difference anyway? she wondered.

Her son, David, came onto the porch as she stood there, tall and gangly like his father, with the same orange hair and blue eyes. He had sported a beard in his junior year in college, which he had shaved off a month ago. Now he kissed her perfunctorily and stared at the cigar.

"Talked him out of it? Can I take it and finish it? It's a shame to waste it."

"No, you cannot."

"OK, OK, just asking."

"Do you want dinner? The fridge is full."

"You're not eating at home?"

"No, we're dining with the Castles."

"Oh?"

"What does that mean?"

"Nothing, nothing at all. You're touchy."

"Am I?" Then she realized that he was quite right. "Well, perhaps. We had a few words about the Castles."

David nodded.

"And you're not to add to it. Do you have a date tonight?"

"I'm taking Nellie to dinner. I have seven dollars left out of my week's pay, which creates a problem. Now, if you're in the mood to negotiate a small loan?"

"I'm not."

"Heart of stone," he muttered. "Who's going to be at the Castles'?"

"Harold Sellig, among others. That's how I got your dad to agree."

"Mom, work me in, please. I'll bring Nellie. I've been looking for Sellig's new book, *The Assassin,* ever since I first read the early draft he sent Dad. I've called Diane's Books and I've driven the old gentleman at Just Books half crazy. Two bookstores in a town of this size, and both of them small—can you imagine? Now, if I can talk to Sellig—"

"It's not my dinner party, and from what I hear the book hasn't been published yet."

"I wonder why? Anyway, how about tonight?"

"No way. Forget it," she said firmly.

Mary kissed him, and then she went into the house and upstairs to change. Herb was tucking the tails of a blue striped shirt into his gray flannels.

Searching through her closet for a dress to wear that evening, she told Herb of her conversation with David. "What shall I wear?" she wondered.

"Anything you can cover with a sweater. They keep that stupid house of theirs cold as an igloo. So he's going out with Nellie Kadinsky. She's something."

"She's a decent, hardworking young woman. And what's 'something'?"

"Blond hair, real; blue eyes, cute."

"I hate that word. Oh, never mind, forgive me. I have nothing to wear. You know, Herb, I've gone through life being a 'non-cute,' to coin a word."

"Have I ever complained?"

"Teachers don't wear dresses." She held up a pink dress. "Do you like this? He tried to touch me for a loan, claims he has only seven dollars for his date tonight. The boy's a senior at Harvard, almost top of his class, and they pay him six dollars an hour to scrape barnacles and paint boats."

"That's good pay," Herb said. "More than I ever got at his age."

He studied his wife as she slipped into the pink dress. It was loose and very simple, hanging from her shoulders, gathered with a sash at the waist. He enjoyed watching her, seeing her, being around her—never entirely used to the fact that she had put up with him for thirty years, good years most of them, put up with his cigars, his cantankerous nature, his bitter wit, his unwillingness to have more than two children, his refusal at the very beginning to be married by a priest, his agnosticism—and for all of that, he had agreed, with almost no argument that she could raise both their children as Catholics, though David now chose to be a Jew. He bridled when someone compared her to the Kennedy women; he had no love for the Kennedys, but she did have the same high-bridged, strong nose and jaw, the same almost-ebony eyes and hair and long-boned frame; and he believed firmly that she and all the other black Irish were descended from the Spanish sailors stranded on their shore when the Armada was destroyed. He had corresponded with a noted Spanish historian, who held that there was no one in Spain who did not have a cupful of Jewish blood, even though as a linguist he was an enemy of that kind of thinking and as a Jew he was lackadaisical at best and immune to all of Mary's arguments that a man could not live properly with no religion at all. When he first met her, at an undergraduate mixer at Harvard, she had said, "I'm Mary O'Brien," to which he responded, "I'm Herb Greene, and I'm Jewish," to which she said, "Thank God, and I'm glad you got that off your chest."

"That dress is wonderful," he said, now in Greenwich thirty years later. "Absolutely wonderful."

"I have a cashmere sweater that goes with it. You're right. The Castles do live in an igloo."

Two

Frank Manelli drove his truck along the Castle driveway and parked in front of the Castle's four-car garage at exactly 5:30. The Castle estate, as Richard Castle liked to call it, consisted of only five acres, but the very large house that dominated that five acres was commonly known as The Castle in the Back Country. The Back Country in Greenwich is that part of the township which lies to the north of the Merritt Parkway. While there are several other enclaves in Greenwich where the very wealthy live, none are as large or as consistently wealthy as the Back Country area.

Manelli was headed for the servants' entrance when Sally Castle emerged from the kitchen door, exclaiming, "Thank God, thank God! Oh, Frank, I was ready to put my head in the oven and end it all. I called you at ten, I called you at twelve." She was bereaved, but not angry. Sally Castle was Richard Castle's second wife, his trophy wife, as it was put around town; but if someone had called her that to her face, she would have smiled and nodded; she had once told Mary Greene she did not mind the appellation, although in truth, she resented it.

Sally was good-natured to a fault, and gentle. At nearly forty, she was still lovely to look at, slender and long-legged with strawberry blond hair that fell to her shoulders and fine blue eyes. Herb had once remarked to Mary that Sally had been gifted with everything but brains, and she was proof that one could survive very well in our society with an IQ of 90 or so. She had once whispered to Mary that she had never stayed in school long enough to take an IQ test and Mary had asked her not to mention it to anyone else.

Richard Castle had a son, Dickie, by his first wife, who had left him and the child for an adequate sum of money and a house in California. She told him to keep his money or shove it up his ass, yet she took it, spending most of it on liquor and dope. The marriage to Sally was now seven years old, and Sally still appeared to adore Richard and still basked in his approval. Sally was a Valley Girl, born and beach-trained in California, married and divorced in turn by a director and then by an actor. When she faced unsolvable problems or the minor disasters that on occasion daunted her, she fell into a pleading, beseeching manner that some men found irresistible.

Frank Manelli did not find it irresistible. "I know, I know," he said, "but I start my day with a program, Mrs. Castle. I try to give everyone a time. But it's like when you go to the dentist. He tells you nine o'clock, and then he got a patient in his chair with twenty cavities. I never know what I'm gonna find, maybe easy, maybe two hours' work." He was a large, burly man in a stained T-shirt, and Sally would shudder a bit with the thought of anyone going to bed with that huge mass of bone and muscle.

"But you are here, thank God," Sally said.

"Where is it?"

"The powder room. That's why I was so disturbed. My powder room. We have six guests coming to dinner tonight, and my powder room is an obscenity. I'm almost ashamed to show it to you."

Manelli hefted his bag of tools, stepped over to his truck, and reached in for a plunger. Then he followed Sally Castle to the front door and into the house. The entry was broad and spacious, the powder-room door to the left as one entered; a trickle of water coming through under the door.

"Josie, Josie," Sally wailed.

Josie, a wan young black woman in a maid's uniform, came running to her call.

"Get some towels, please, Josie, and stop that dreadful stuff before it reaches the rug." And to Manelli, "Can you just go in without me, Frank. I can't stand the smell. It's the toilet. I tell them not to use the powder room, but they do."

Manelli nodded, but waited a moment until Josie returned with an armful of towels. He took one from her and entered the powder room, closing the door behind him. His guess had been correct; the toilet had overflowed, and there were soft feces on the floor. He sighed, drove the plunger into the toilet several times, heard the suction break, and watched the water run down. He flushed the toilet, using the plunger as the water ran into the bowl. Then he used the towel to gather the mess. He flushed the toilet again to make certain that it was working properly. Then he stood in the powder room for a long moment, regarding his face in the mirror.

"Shit," he said softly. "Shit and more shit."

Josie was still mopping the floor when he emerged from the powder room, plunger in hand.

"Did you fix it?" Sally pleaded.

No, he thought, no, she didn't do this to fuck you out of your mind. She's got to be thirty-five or more, and she don't know how a fuckin' toilet works.

"I fixed it," he said. "Someone dropped a sanitary napkin or a paper diaper into the toilet. You can't do that with this toilet."

"But, Frank, we have no infants here."

He shrugged and held up the plunger. "You know what this is?"

She shook her head.

"OK. I'll show Josie how to use it. I'll leave it in the kitchen. I'll bring this towel in there."

She nodded. "Thank you, Frank. You saved my life."

He knew where the kitchen was. He knew everything in the house that had water running through it. What he didn't expect to find in the kitchen was Abel Hunt, working at the huge eight-burner stove.

"Fired?" he asked Abel. "Or did you switch to cooking for the rich?"

"I always cook for the rich. The poor can't afford decent food, much less cooks."

"I'm covered with shit," Frank said sourly. "Where can I wash?"

"Try that sink over there," he said, pointing. "The club is having a 'Japanese Night' with a special chef doing the honors, so I pick up a few bucks off the books here and there."

Abel Hunt was a big man, six foot two inches and weighing in at two hundred and fifty pounds, a black man, dark as coal. The Hunts lived four houses away from the Manellis, in a section of Greenwich township called Chickahominy, a neighborhood that would have rated as decently lower middle anywhere else but in Greenwich, and where in the lunatic real-estate market of the nineties, a house could still be purchased for less than half a million dollars, and a black family or two could be found.

Hunt had been born in South Carolina, which in his opinion, gastronomically speaking, was the first state in the Union. At Chapel Hill, he had refused a football scholarship, graduated among the top ten in his class, working his way through college as a short-order cook; and then, refusing an offer from General Motors to become what he called "a well-paid showcase nigger," he had taken off for Paris via a thousand-dollar scholastic prize and enrolled himself at the Cordon Bleu. He supported himself with nightclub gigs, playing a tin whistle, and it was there that he met Delia, a lovely coffee-colored singer from New Orleans, whom he married.

Offered a job as a pastry chef at the Hill Crest Club in Greenwich, he accepted it. Now, twenty years later, he was head chef at a salary of seventy thousand a year.

Frank Manelli was drying his hands at the sink when Josie came into the kitchen wing with her mess of wet towels. Frank handed her the plunger, telling her to keep it handy. "You get a toilet won't flush down, Josie, just drive this plunger into it, slow and firm. That'll save me a trip out here to the Back Country."

Josie nodded. Both Abel Hunt and his assistant, Joseph, his nineteen-year-old son, who had just finished his first year as a pre-med student at Harvard, were smiling—slightly it must be said—and Frank said to them softly, "I don't like these people no better than you, Abel, but Jesus, to just let that toilet flush the shit all over the floor—"

"I'm a cook." Abel shrugged. "Anyway, there isn't a plunger in this whole stupid house. And I don't use the powder room."

Frank nodded and sighed. He had been through a long, hard day, and by now, every muscle in his body ached. All he could think of was to get home, take a hot shower, and have dinner. He liked Abel, the only black man he had made a friend of since Vietnam, where you made friends of black men and sometimes died with them; and anyway, they were neighbors and went to church with their kids, and he was not going to be pissed off because Abel had not foreseen that he would be called to fix the goddamn toilet.

"I'm sorry, Frank," Abel said. "The truth is, I didn't know about the powder room until after she called you, and she's a nice lady but—you know."

"I know." Frank picked up his bag of tools and went out through the kitchen door. As he opened the door of his truck, Richard Castle drove up in his two-seater Mercedes, and called out to him, "Hold on a moment, Frank."

Frank waited for Castle, anticipating that he would offer to pay in cash. Richard Castle always liked to do business with service in cash.

"Nothing serious, I hope," Castle said. It was Friday, and he always drove to New York on Friday. He was a slender, handsome man, wearing his sixties well, a good head of white hair and blue eyes that sent a false message of innocence.

"No, not serious. A stuffed toilet in the powder room."

"Fixed, is it?"

"Yes." Frank had a problem with Castle. The man had always treated him decently, so Frank struggled with the stories he had heard, and none of them were good.

Now Castle put his hand in his pocket, took out a money clip full of bills, and asked Frank, "What do I owe you?"

"I haven't made out a bill yet. No hurry."

"Money doesn't wait, Frank. That's the trouble with you guys. Trusting." He grinned. "I wouldn't trust my own mother. Come to think of it, I never did." He peeled off two fifty-dollar bills from the wad in the money clip. "They look phony, but they're real. Some jerk in Washington decided on the new design," he said, handing the bills to Frank. "Does this cover it?"

Frank shook his head. "Too much. Why don't I send you a bill?" He was trying to recall what a plunger cost—five dollars perhaps, no more.

"Because my time for writing out the check is worth more— Oh, the hell with it, Frank. Take the money and run."

Sally was calling him from the house. "The master calls," Castle said, turning on his heel and striding toward the front door.

Frank climbed into his truck. Switching on the ignition,

he looked at the two bills, still crushed in his hand. His hand was shaking with repressed anger, and at the same time he was telling himself that he had no reason to be angry. It was thirty minutes of driving back to Chickahominy, almost two hours if he counted the round-trip. Fuck Castle! He didn't want to come home angry and face his wife angry. This kind of idiocy was worth a hundred dollars, and like Castle's brain-damaged wife, Castle hadn't pulled his small stunt to put Frank down. In Castle's mind, it was a gift that Frank could stuff into his pocket and use as he pleased.

Back in the huge white-enamel and stainless-steel kitchen, Abel Hunt was telling his son, "No, no, no. You do not make dressing in my kitchen with a Waring blender. You whip it by hand. Otherwise, mayonnaise is not mayonnaise. It's inflated junk."

"Pop," Joseph said, "why do you hate technology?"

"I don't hate technology. I love cooking. I love good food. Good food distinguishes us from the barbarians among whom we live. Technology has nothing to do with cooking. Technology, in its broadest sense, simply substitutes an M16 for the pilum."

"What on earth is a pilum?"

"Oh, that's beautiful!" Abel snorted. "Just beautiful! I spend my hard-earned money and lifelong skills to send my son to Harvard to prove that a dying, corroding mass of white Protestants can depend on us to take over and run things properly, and he asks me, What is a pilum?"

"Is this what you want me to use on the mayonnaise?" asked Joseph, holding up a wire whip. "And by the way, I'm pre-med, and they feed it to you slowly. We're not up to the pilum yet."

"Yes, and whip light and even. God help us, if that's what education is today! The pilum was the Roman weapon that conquered the world, a javelin six-foot long— three feet of wood, very heavy, and then a soft iron shaft with a steel point. It was thrown at close range, cut through shield and armor and into the body, and then the weight of the wooden part bent the soft iron, so that even if the soldier was not killed, his shield was useless."

"I don't believe this," his son said.

"Of course, you don't. You want this old nigger to be just as ignorant as his great grandfather. Please watch what you're doing—round strokes."

"Who was your great grandfather?" Joseph asked.

"A field hand. You don't want a froth. You want a dressing."

Three

Ruth Ferguson Sellig, Harold Sellig's wife, was Sally Castle's close friend. Sally had few friends. She played neither tennis nor golf, had limited graces, and never knew what to say in terms of conversation. With a small vocabulary, she fell into gaffs, such as substituting *unsuitable* for *unstable,* and her obvious blond beauty was threatening to the Back Country club crowd. Ruth Sellig had encountered her at a charity affair at a time when Ruth was working on a *Vanity Fair* spread on Marilyn Monroe look-alikes. Ruth asked Sally whether she could photograph her, and Sally was delighted, although with the caveat that she had to ask permission from her husband, Richard.

With such permission readily granted, she became a frequent model for Ruth Sellig, which not only earned her pocket money but found her someone she could talk to. Ruth, an easy mark for any stray, came to like Sally; and although Sally was near forty, old enough to be Ruth's sister, the relationship was curiously mother and daughter. Ruth became a sort of confessor. When, for example, Sally told her that she used to go to bed with men because she could think of no other reason for them to like her, Ruth neither snorted nor laughed, but instead managed to convince Sally of her beauty and desirability.

It was through this relationship that Ruth and Harold Sellig came to know the Castles. They, the Selligs, lived in Riverside, a part of Greenwich that was a full five miles from the edge of the Back Country. Possibly no town in Connecticut was as sharply divided in attitude and political thinking as Greenwich, Connecticut. Nevertheless, Harold Sellig went willingly when invited to dinner at the Castles. As he put it, he knew only half a dozen millionaires, and since they had become a large and significant part of the American scene, they were worth observing.

Sellig was ten years older than his wife's forty-eight. But in mind and impulse, they were very much alike, perhaps as much alike as a Jew born in Brooklyn and a Presbyterian born in Greenwich could be. They had one son, Oscar, just turned eighteen, and now wandering around Europe before beginning his freshmen year at college.

The day before, Ruth's father, Dr. Seth Ferguson, a widower who was one of the few remaining independent family practitioners in Greenwich, had put himself into Greenwich Hospital with chest pains. Today, he was scheduled for a three-way bypass, and the morning of the dinner at the Castles', Ruth informed her husband that she would spend most of the day and perhaps overnight as well with her father at the hospital.

"So you'll have to go it alone at the Castles'."

"I could get out of it and be with you at the hospital."

"No. Sally expects you, and they've invited Professor Greene because you always said you'd like to meet him—"

"Of course! I feel rotten not being with you, but Greene. I always wanted to meet him, and you're only a telephone call away. If you want me there, I'll be there in a few minutes. Anyway, I sent Greene a copy of my manuscript. Maybe by now he's read it."

She shook her head. "I have absolute confidence in the surgeon, and Pop says it's a lark. I'd know if he were worried, and he's not. It will be sitting there and waiting, and that can be a dreadful bore and worry, but I must be there."

"Of course."

"Do you have something for me to read?"

"Yes, the manuscript! I think I finished it. I was working on it until midnight."

"Oh no." Ruth sighed. "You mean 'The Assassin.' Hal, you've been manicuring that whatever-it-is for years. I've read it twice. It will never be published, and it has nothing whatsoever to do with Greenwich."

"I've had three best-sellers. They'll publish the telephone directory with my name on it as long as they can charge enough. But it's a hundred and twenty pages. It's not a novel and it's not an essay."

"Exactly. And it has nothing to do with Greenwich."

"But it has everything to do with Greenwich, with America—with where the hell we've been and where we're going."

"If you think so. I'll read it again."

"I made changes. Read it, please—if only as an assault on boredom. Do it for me. I ask a small favor."

"And see myself as that skinny demented Wasp in your book?"

Harold had begun his opus with a title: "The Assassin." He had a sort of theory, which he took from a slogan of the National Rifle Association, "Guns don't kill people. People kill people," and enlarged it to include assassins—assassins and guns are not separable; the two are one.

His theory was that the killers who carried out the endless round of assassinations and murders which had marked his adulthood years, murders of obscure people who never entered the public mind until they had been killed, as well as the murders of national and international luminaries, such as John Kennedy and Robert Kennedy and Martin Luther King Jr., and Mahatma Gandhi, were not the basic cause of the action of assassination but the result of the desire of well-to-do and comfortable people who lived orderly and lawful lives—such as so many people in Greenwich did—to continue to live their lives in the manner they did. This raised a problem for Ruth, and they had discussed it to the point of Ruth's utter boredom.

But then, when he began to write, leaning on the proposition that Greenwich and similar places defined American society, Ruth pointed out to him that he had lost Greenwich. He was writing the story of an assassin.

"That," he said, "is precisely it."

"But decent people do not employ assassins."

"Who else does?"

His wife, Ruth, had been privy to this meandering mental excursion he had embarked on, and it was through her that he met not only some of the assortment of CEOs who had chosen Greenwich as their living space, but also a variety of Wall Street millionaires and even one or two billionaires, as well as politicians and highly placed United Nations officials, both American and foreign, Greenwich being a favorite spot for UN officials to settle their families while they did their work in New York.

But while Ruth had been privy to all of this, and even aided it with her knowledge of Greenwich and her father's connections, she by no means shared his theory. She rested secure in the belief that the manuscript would never see the light of print.

Their relationship was one of mutual respect. She was a successful photographer, he was a successful writer, and they enjoyed each other, both body and mind. And the never-completed manuscript gave Harold a hobby, since he had absolutely no interest in golf or tennis or gardening or any other manner of physical exercise.

Now, however, he was delighted that she would be taking the latest version of his manuscript with her to read during the hours she would have to spend at Greenwich Hospital.

Harold was inordinately fond of Ruth's father, Dr. Ferguson, who like himself, was a cigar smoker and beer drinker. "Good beer," he had once explained to Harold, "is not an alcoholic beverage. It's food as old as mankind. It's mother's milk for those poor bastards we call blue-collar workers, and it's beneficial to the urinary system."

Harold was relieved to hear from Ruth that her father was not worried about the surgery, and he decided that the day after the operation, he would keep the older man company at the hospital.

Four

When Frank Manelli walked into his home that evening, his wife, Constance, took one look at him, made no move toward her usual welcoming kiss, but said immediately, "Sit down, Frank, and let off some steam, and I'll get you a cold beer."

"I don't want to sit down, I don't want a beer, I don't even want to talk. I want to get into a hot bath and sit there."

"Sure," Constance said quickly. She was a round gentle woman, round not fat, who counted her blessings and was satisfied with them. She had started to go with Frank when both of them were students at Greenwich High School, and now there were four kids with Frankie Junior going into his sophomore year at UConn and Dorothy beginning in the fall as a freshman at Sacred Heart University, and the two younger ones still at Greenwich High—all this on the income of an independent working plumber. Frank could have put young Frank on the truck with him, and he and Constance had discussed this, but when the boy said he wanted a degree in engineering, Frank supported him all the way.

Not that Frank ever put himself down as a plumber. In a good year, he netted better than sixty thousand dollars, which was all right but only barely met their needs with four kids; and he also took pride in the fact that civilization, or at least a great deal of it, would come to an end without his ministrations.

Unlike so many of his neighbors in the Chickahominy section of Greenwich, Frank never took out his frustrations on those he loved, nor did he leave the church to his wife and children. He was unhappily aware of his own lack of education, having left school to go to work at age sixteen, and he tried to get to every lecture at St. Matthew's that dealt with any kind of behavioral knowledge. In particular, he took to heart an evening where Monsignor Donovan dealt with rage and the habit of inflicting rage and anger on those we love—the point being that inflicted elsewhere it would not be tolerated. He thought about that now as he lay in a tub of hot water, letting his tight muscles relax. He had all the bodily pains of a heavily muscled middle-aged man, each part of his body knotting up as he twisted into the variety of positions his work required.

He heard the door open, and Constance asking softly, "Want me to rub your back, Frank?"

"Yeah—thanks."

She loved her husband and never stopped thanking God for him, and she was proud of his large tight body, not a bit of fat anywhere, no beer belly, just hard muscle under the white skin. She soaped and rubbed his back.

"Not a good day, Frank?"

"A lousy day. I spent three hours in a crawl space forty-eight inches high. The house sold for a million two, from what the agent told me, and they put the water connections in a crawl space, or built over them, or whatever. In this demented town, they buy a shack and turn it into a million plus. It must have been a hundred and ten degrees in there, in Belle Haven, about a mile from here, and then I had to drive to the other end of the Back Country, where this stupid bitch, Castle's wife, had a powder room full of wet shit because she didn't know what a toilet plunger was—"

"Frank!"

"Yeah. I'm sorry. I hate the word, too, but I live with it."

"Frankie, think of Mr. Lombardy, who has to drive his truck around and suck out the septic tanks."

"I don't want to think about it—not before dinner. And then that piece of—all right, crap—she's married to drives up in his seventy-five-thousand Mercedes convertible, and he shoves two fifty-dollar bills at me. Not that the job wasn't worth a hundred dollars—just the stupidity of the whole idiot thing was worth a hundred—but when I say, No, I'll send him a bill, he won't take that but shoves the two fifties at me, grinning, because he thinks I'm a lousy Italian mafioso or something and just as crooked as he is, and I can take this off the books and cheat the feds the way he does with his millions—that lousy little bastard! I don't grudge him his stinking millions but it's calling me a goddamn thief—I swear, I could have decked him on the spot—"

"Frank!"

"I didn't. I just drove off."

"I'll send him a bill and mark it paid, Frank, and that will tell him where we stand, and I'll deposit the money."

"And he'll put me down as a shmuck."

"Frankie, Frankie, you got more sense in your little finger than he has in his whole head. I'll put your clothes in the washer—"

"The money's in my pocket."

"—I'll take it out. It's a warm evening—how about shorts and a T-shirt?"

"You read my mind."

"I'll bring them. We have orzo and greens and sausage for dinner."

"Great."

"Christina won't be here for dinner. She has a date."

"Come on, she's too young for dates."

"Frank, she's fifteen and she'll be sixteen when school starts in the fall. This is nothing. They're going to have pizza and then see *Godzilla,* and she'll be back early."

"Who's the boy?"

"She says he's a nice kid."

"What's his name?"

"She said Dick. I didn't ask her. For heaven's sake, Frank, it's pizza and a movie. She's not going to marry him."

Five

Driving out to the Castles' home in the Back Country, Sister Pat Brody told Monsignor Donovan that she had difficulty in accepting the basis of their errand.

"It is not an errand, Sister. It is a dinner invitation, and you are invited because Mrs. Castle may want to talk about matters that might make her uncomfortable speaking to a man. We are going to arrive a bit early, before the other guests, so that you can have at least a few minutes alone with her."

"But why does she come to us? Why not to St. Michael's, so much closer to the Back Country, or to St. Mary's on Greenwich Avenue?"

"She is a very timid woman, and lives, I venture to say, in some fear, if not terror, of her husband. She doesn't dare go to St. Michael's because some of her husband's friends might recognize her, and I don't think she even knew that St. Mary's is a Catholic church. She chose St. Matthew's because it is at the extreme opposite end of Greenwich, and when she spoke to Father Garibaldi, he was just out of his depth and brought her to me. She is also very beautiful."

"Which is the bottom line to most men!" Sister Brody, a plump woman with a sharp tongue, never stood on ceremony with priests.

"Yes, Sister, I'm afraid so. God made us that way."

"I'm glad none of our parishioners are listening to this conversation. I still don't understand."

"Then consider our Secretary of State, who thought she was born a Catholic, until someone discovered that she was born Jewish."

"That was the result of the Holocaust. It's not comparable. You say this woman is about forty?"

"Yes. A guess. I didn't ask her," Donovan replied, somewhat defensively.

"And you tell me that she believes that perhaps she is a Catholic? Or does she want to convert? Was she baptized?"

"She doesn't know."

"But how was she raised?"

"Like a stray dog, from all I could gather. She has lied so much about her past that apparently she cannot separate invention from reality. She calls herself a Valley Girl, which is very pejorative in Southern California. She doesn't know who her mother and father are, and she confessed to me that she had invented them. I don't know that anyone will ever know the truth of her background, but there's nothing bitter in her nature, but a certain kind of innocence. She used the word *tramp* in describing herself to me, but I don't know. I hate the word, and perhaps she felt that by talking to a priest she could plumb some inner feeling that she was unable to reveal even to herself."

"You didn't confess her?"

"No, no, no, we simply talked. I don't know whether she even knows what confession is, and her notions of Catholi-

cism are confused, to put it in the best light. But she has no
anchor and she lives in an environment—well, you'll see
for yourself tonight. She is also, as I said, afraid of the man
she's married to."

"What is he like?" Sister Brody asked, her tone of voice
changing.

"What is he like?" Monsignor Donovan repeated.

"I presume he's not a Catholic?"

"No. When they go to church, Christmas once and
Easter once, they go to Christ Church, but from what she
said, he has no affiliation with the Episcopalians or anywhere else. She said that some of his business friends go to
Christ Church. Christ Church—well, she thought it was a
Catholic church, and when she mentioned that to him, he
became very angry."

"Poor child. What do you imagine—or what does she
imagine—he would do if she were to be baptized as a
Catholic?"

"I asked her that, more or less. She thinks he would kill
her—possibly hyperbole, but she is afraid. In any case, he
would throw her out, which at this point in her life might
amount to the same thing."

"Surely there was a prenuptial agreement," Sister Brody
said. She was a practical person.

"Yes. She knows she signed some sort of agreement, but
she doesn't know what she signed, nor was she represented
by an attorney. She's not very bright, Sister, and don't lecture me on feminism. She is simply not very bright. My
guess is that the premarital agreement gave her nothing."

"I can't imagine that any lawyer who isn't completely a
scoundrel would agree to draw up anything like that."

"Lawyers are like other people, and there are scoundrels,
and money will buy advice for sale."

"Then what hope is there for Mrs. Castle?"

"I don't know. That's why I depend on your very per-
ceptive and keen intelligence."

"Or else you're using me as a cop-out. Which is it, Monsignor? If she decides that she wants to join the church, well, where do we go from there? Wreck her marriage, which is still better than sleeping in the street, or maybe get her killed by the man she's married to? Haven't we enough trouble? And it's not even our parish. Just suppose that she decides to take on the church and that her husband can be talked into it. Oh, they'll love that at St. Michael's, taking the wife of a Back Country millionaire and dragging her off to money-strapped St. Matthew's—another parish."

"Sister, a practical turn of mind is one thing, but you don't turn away a human being pleading for help."

"Please don't lecture me, Monsignor. I will talk to her and we'll see. But I will not push her into the church, and I will ask her to consider the consequences to her personal life."

The monsignor did not reply to that, thinking that in Sister Brody, he might well have taken on more than he had bargained for.

Six

Richard Bush Castle was related neither to the Bush who had been president some years back nor to the family that had once owned Bush-Holley House, a small period museum in Greenwich, built some two centuries ago by a Jew who liked the notion of living in Greenwich. Castle's family had put no middle name on his birth certificate, so he simply appropriated the name "Bush," an action legal in Connecticut. He felt that it gave him style and importance.

In the normal course of things, he certainly would never have asked Monsignor Donovan to dinner. He disliked Catholics, with passion and undisguised contempt. As he had put it once to Sally, "They're worse than Jews. They all belong body and soul to the Vatican, and their endgame is to take over!" His own religious roots, if they could be called that, were small-town Baptist, but he had discarded that in years past, leaving them in the Georgia village where he had been born. He was shrewd, cunning without foresight, but bright enough to get through Georgetown University, to get a job in government, and to work himself up to a spot in the Reagan administration as Assistant Secretary for Latin American Affairs.

He moved to Greenwich in 1982, abandoned the government—because there was no money in it—and became an investment banker and money trader. During the nineties, he blossomed in the financial world.

Thus, when Sally asked a question that would have evoked a storm of anger from him at another time—whether she could invite Monsignor Donovan to the dinner party—he agreed, deciding that it was better to know why a monsignor might desire to see him than to wonder how much anyone in Greenwich knew about certain incidents during his time with the State Department. It never occurred to him that a priest might be interested in Sally's problems, or that Sally had any problems besides running the house and playing the role of a more-beautiful-than-usual trophy wife.

His willingness to see Father Donovan stemmed from his desire to find out just how much Father Donovan knew about him; and since the monsignor worked at a parish at the opposite end of Greenwich, Richard felt he could control whatever knowledge there was.

All of this stemmed from a story in the *New York Times,* which began:

"El Salvador's defense minister suspected that a member of his high command had ordered the killing of four American churchwomen in 1980 and later informed the U.S. ambassador of his belief, according to newly released State Department documents. . . ." And then it went on to say that "Three Roman Catholic nuns, Maura Clarke, Ita Ford and Dorothy Kazel, and a lay worker, Jean Donovan, were abducted by a military unit on Dec. 2, 1980, and raped and shot to death."

The story was a long one, and Castle had read it carefully and then reread it several times. He had vivid memories of those times, of a meeting in Washington where a decision had been made to "get rid of those Jesuit bastards once and for all." And while he had not been alone in ordering the killings of these particular churchwomen and the other killings of Jesuits that followed, he alone had signed on to the instructions written in detail and his name was on numerous documents, as well as one that discussed the assassination of the bishop of the central church in El Salvador.

As long as the Soviet Union was in existence, he knew that these assassinations would be filed as part of the battle against communism; but with the Soviet Union a thing of the past, and with more and more of these stories coming to light, Richard Castle's uneasiness had increased. Now, with a major story on the affair in the *New York Times,* he felt that he must try to find out what was in store for him locally, and therefore he had agreed to Sally's suggestion that the monsignor be invited to dinner.

When Sister Brody and Monsignor Donovan arrived, both Richard and Sally welcomed them cordially. Richard took the monsignor around the grounds, making a point of the new swimming pool, just completed, forty-eight feet in length to replace the thirty-eight-foot pool that had been there, explaining that it was no easy matter to stay in shape with a short pool.

"Although why it had to cost two hundred thousand dollars when most of the excavation was already dug, I don't know. Of course, the old masonry had to be scrapped. One of the disadvantages of being rich is that you get soaked for everything, don't you think so?"

"I'm hardly the one to ask. I've never been rich."

"Yes. Sure." He swallowed any thought of asking the cleric what his job paid.

"I'll show you the gardens," Richard said, at his wit's end for a subject. "I had them redone completely by Tony Compana. He has an international reputation, and this, he tells me, is a seventeenth-century Florentine layout, except that the hedges are English. When the tour comes around"—referring to the annual charity tour of Greenwich houses of the super rich—"I always lead them through the gardens myself. After all, it's charity. I always accept my obligations to charity. This, over here, is agapanthus and these topiary specimens cost an arm and a leg. I grew up on a farm, I mean sort of, we lived on the edge of town. But we grew plants, didn't buy them in a nursery . . ."

While Richard was struggling with the monsignor and praying that the other guests would soon arrive and take him off the hook and listening at the same time for any hint that the priest knew something about the El Salvador business, Sally was leading Sister Brody around the house, pointing out what she called "nice things," and mentioning, on occasion, with awe, their price. When they reached her bedroom, Sally sighed and shook her head.

"Why don't we sit down here and talk?" Sister Brody suggested. "It's so pretty and cool."

"Yes. Sure. Can I get you a cold drink?"

"Don't trouble, please."

"It's no trouble. I just press a button and they'll bring me anything I want. I'd just as soon go down to the kitchen or the bar and get it myself, but this is the way Richard wants it done. I do everything the way Richard wants it done. He's very good to me—I mean when he's not angry."

"I don't want anything, dear. When the other guests come, I'm sure there'll be drinks and things to nibble, but now I'd just like to sit here and chat." Sister Brody wore a pale gray skirt and a loose white blouse. Sally was relieved that she wasn't wearing one of those heavy, hooded things that some nuns, she supposed, had to wear.

"What shall I call you?" Sally asked uneasily.

"You can call me Pat or Sister Pat or whatever."

"That's nice. Thank you."

Sister Pat rearranged her thinking, sitting and looking at this exquisitely beautiful woman and trying to find an inkling of what was inside of her. Pat Brody was far from being a cloistered nun. She had dealt with women whose husbands had beat them to a pulp, and with women expecting a fifth child with no way of feeding the previous four, and with women whose husbands had walked out and away from every responsibility. She had worked in Guatemala and in El Salvador as well as in the worst slums of New York and Philadelphia; but this was something else entirely.

Now she said to Sally, "I think we should talk about religion. You know, of course, that I'm a Catholic nun. I am what they call a Sister of Charity. I don't live in a convent. I work with people who need help with social and religious problems, a sort of social worker you might say. I am explaining this because I know you haven't had much experience about how the church works. That's why Monsignor brought me here to meet you and talk with you."

"I understand," Sally said.

"Do you believe in God, Sally?"

"Oh, yes—yes, of course."

"Then something must have influenced you in that belief. Do you know what religion your parents had?"

Sally shook her head.

"Are they still alive, my dear?"

Sally hesitated, and then said straightforwardly, "I tell lies. If I tell you the truth, will you promise not to tell Richard?"

Sister Brody nodded. "Absolutely—I promise."

"I don't know who my parents are."

"How did that happen?"

"I don't know. When I was two or three years old, I'm not sure, a Mexican family in the Simi Valley found me in an irrigation ditch. They kept me for two years, I think, but they weren't nice to me and I ran away. The police picked me up, as near as I could remember, but no one reported me missing. Most of that part is very confused, and I don't remember it very well. They put me in an orphanage, and I went to school and learned to read—and I ran away. No one wanted to adopt me because I was sickly. I got rides to Los Angeles, and I met men who gave me money and I guess I was sort of a hooker—is this like a confession?"

"No, my dear. I'm not a priest. We're just talking. Now I must ask you something. This Mexican family that found you in the irrigation ditch, did they have you baptized?"

Sally shrugged. "I don't know."

"And you were never baptized at any other time?"

"No."

Sister Brody took a deep breath, spent a moment or two in silence, and then said, "Here is what I would suggest— providing that you have thought about being a Catholic and would like to take the step?"

Sally nodded.

"You're sure?"

"Oh yes, I'm sure."

"Then we will arrange for you to take instructions. Father Donovan will take care of it. He celebrates mass every day at St. Matthew's. The baptism, after you've completed the instructions, is a simple and beautiful ceremony, and then, if you want to go on with it and join our church, we will arrange that for you. Now I must tell you that in the normal course of things, you would go to St. Michael's, which is the parish church for this area. But there's no reason why you shouldn't choose St. Matthew's, and I understand why you might be more comfortable there."

"Must I tell my husband?"

"No, not if you don't want to, and what you have said to me remains with me. And any time you want to talk to me, call me at the church or leave a message for me."

Abel Hunt's son, Joseph, 4.0 average through his freshman year at Harvard, pre-med, sat at the kitchen computer—it was Richard Castle's boast that his was the first kitchen in Greenwich with its own computer—printing out the menus. He observed to his father that this kind of thing might permanently impair the neural structure of his brain. "I don't know," Joseph said, "whether I am crazy or the rest of the world is crazy."

"Both," Abel replied shortly. "You're on vacation. I do this all year round on every night off. I get four hundred dollars for cooking dinner for some demented Greenwich millionaire. That's the world you live in."

"Yes. And in Boston, there's an old black lady who spends the winter on an iron grate, because some hot air seeps up through it. I give her a dollar when I can get there. I came there once, and she had six inches of snow over her."

"She doesn't have three kids in college on a chef's salary."

"I'm on scholarship."

"That's your payoff for being a smart-ass nigger. Your sisters are normal, not smart-ass."

"I hate that word."

"Then don't use it."

"I don't. Let me go over this before I print it out. First course: crabmeat ravigote." He spelled it out. "Is that right?"

"Seems to be."

"Second course, trout amandine with beurre blanc and capers. I spell it *a-m-a-n-d-i-n-e*—right?"

"I keep reading," Abel said, "about these poor little black kids a kind and gentle government sends to college and they can't even spell."

"You got me," Joseph replied. "Escalope de veau finished with shallots and white wine. I don't take French. You want to be a doctor in this besotted land, you study Spanish. I'm trying to read your handwriting. Asparagus tips, mélange of baby carrots, zucchini, and pattypan squash. What on earth are pattypan squash?"

"The little white things that look like land mines."

"Risotto with chanterelles, morels, and truffles."

"So far so good," Abel said.

At this point, Josie, the regular Castle cook, had entered the kitchen and was listening with all the admiration she felt for her occasional substitute and his good-looking son.

"Mesclun salad with fresh raspberries and raspberry vinaigrette. Dessert—tarte Tatin, crème fraîche, chocolate-dipped sorbet berries. How do I put in this business of grapefruit gratinée with fresh mint? Can I just print it at the bottom?"

"The bill at Hay Day," Josie snorted, "was larger than my week's pay."

"Not my problem, baby," Abel said, grinning at her.

Seven

You know," Herbert Greene said to his wife, driving across Greenwich from Old Greenwich over and into the Back Country, "he's not going to give you anything for the library. He doesn't know what a library is. He doesn't know what a book is."

"Why must you always be so damn judgmental? You really don't know the man. You've only met him a couple of times."

"He's rich, he's pretentious, he's ignorant, and he beat the shit out of his last wife."

"How do you know that?"

"Seth Ferguson told me about it."

"He shouldn't have."

"Why not? Seth's a doctor, not a priest."

"He treats Sally well."

"Yes, he gets a medal for that."

"Herb," she said firmly, "be nice tonight. I'm asking you to do that for me. Sally is so excited that you agreed to come, and it's going to be interesting. Harold and Ruth Sellig will be there and Monsignor Donovan and Pat Brody—you know her—"

"Come off it! You mean Castle's invited a Catholic priest and a nun to dinner at his house! Come on! Why?"

"Sally invited them. I mean she just brought it up, telling Richard that she happened to run into them, never expecting any positive response from him, and then to her amazement, he said, Sure, invite them to dinner."

"That is really amazing," Herb agreed. "I've heard that Donovan is a brilliant and thoughtful man. All right, you win. I'll be properly behaved and controlled."

"And one more enticing bit. Abel Hunt is cooking the dinner."

"Who is Abel Hunt?"

"You don't know? Of course, you wouldn't know. You abhor the clubs, but I teach at the Central Middle School and I hear things. He's the chef at the Hill Crest Club, and on his night off he'll do dinner for one or another local tycoon. He's cooking for the Castles tonight, and you just might enjoy it."

When Ruth Sellig called Sally Castle, earlier that day, and told her that her father faced a serious operation that same day, Sally was both bewildered and upset. Since all of Sally's attitudes toward a father were theoretical, gleaned for the most part from TV and films, she felt she had to respect Ruth's last-minute cancellation. On the other hand, she knew that Richard would be irritated by an uneven number of dinner guests, and when Richard was irritated, he became mean and directed his venom at Sally. The cause of the venom could be large, small, or nothing at all. Sally rummaged through her acquaintances for a possible replacement, someone who was alone and free this evening and would not let pride stand in the way of such a

last-minute invitation. She did not know too many people
who might stand in for Ruth Sellig; as a matter of fact,
there was only one she could think of, Muffy Platt, whose
husband worked for the Swiss Union Bank and was abroad
in Switzerland most of the time.

And Richard liked Muffy. Once, at the club, Sally had
stumbled on Richard and Muffy in an embrace, with
Richard's hand up her short skirt, fondling her ass, but neither of them noticed Sally and she was able to slip away
unseen, greatly relieved that she did not have to deal with
their awareness of her knowledge. It was not that Sally was
indifferent to this sort of thing on Richard's part; she simply knew no way of responding to it, and therefore she ig-
nored it.

Nor did it change her attitude toward Muffy, even
though it bewildered her. Her two previous Hollywood
marriages were short-lived and cruel. She married because
she so desperately needed to be loved and protected, and she
had used her beauty almost without ever realizing that
she was using it. Once she had spoken to Ruth Sellig about
the incident with Muffy, asking Ruth, "Can I continue to
be her friend?" a question to which Ruth had no answer.

"How can anyone live like that?" Ruth had asked her
husband.

And to that, Harold had no answer.

P eople who knew the Selligs and observed how easily
they lived with each other fell back on the cliché that op-
posites attract, but this was an idle and somewhat obvious
conclusion. Ruth Sellig was tall, slender, and dark, with
dark eyes and close-cropped gray hair. Her features were
well-defined, her nose small, nothing effusive about her,
her brown eyes searching rather than inviting, and only in
her full, wide mouth any hint of passion lying somewhere
in her tight, well-controlled body. Her husband, Harold,
was a full three inches shorter, plump; a sandy mustache;

sandy, whitish hair around a bald pate; good-natured; open to anything and everything; blue eyes peering out of metal-rimmed glasses; originally from Flatbush, Brooklyn; a Rhodes scholar with a sort of English accent, which he had cultivated assiduously after a year at Oxford. He had done a long tour in Vietnam—the most unlikely member of the armed forces ever enlisted—as a naval historian on an aircraft carrier off the coast; and while this resulted in a book, still unpublished, he was somewhat ashamed of the fact that his days ashore amounted to less than a month.

Ruth had remarked to her father that she never spent a boring hour with her husband. Frequently his way of thinking drove her up the wall, but at least it was never the expected.

The manuscript, which he had persuaded her to take with her to the hospital and to read once again while she waited through the hours of the operation, contained the quality of being both the expected and the unexpected—unexpected when she first read it years ago and very much expected now. He had begun to write it after the Vietnam tour was over, and as he explained to her, "I am going to write an autobiography of an assassin, and I am going to call it 'The Assassin,' because no one in Greenwich, which is absolutely a capsule of the United States in every way I can think of, would ever dream of being in the shoes of an assassin."

Her reaction was summed up in one short word, "Oh?"

"Just oh?"

"What else can I say, Hal?"

"You don't think Greenwich is a capsule of the U.S. today?"

"I never thought about it," Ruth replied.

"What is Greenwich?"

"You really want me to play this game with you, Hal?"

"If you will, humor me."

"All right. Greenwich is a town in Connecticut that borders on New York State. It is partly a commuter suburb and

partly a local financial and big-business center. It contains
a number of very rich people, a lot of middle-class people,
and our own share of the poor. It is a well-kept decent town
with excellent schools and a very low crime rate, and no
assassins that I have ever heard of."

"Exactly," Harold said.

Ruth sighed. "And therefore," she said patiently, "you're
going to write the autobiography of an assassin and base it
on Greenwich, Connecticut. Do I follow you?"

"Yes."

"Each to his own," she said, and left it at that.

Then Harold wrote his first draft and Ruth read it. He
asked her whether she had enjoyed it.

"Not very much."

"Do you see why I base it on Greenwich?"

"No," Ruth admitted.

"Look at it this way: There is the gun and there is the
shooter. They add up to a weapon. Each is part and parcel
of the world we live in. Each is nothing without the other.
Both together add up to you and me, and every one of us.
The guilt is collective."

"Oh, Hal, come on! If you want to lay all this Jewish
guilt on yourself, fine—but don't include me. Thank God
I'm a housewife, a mother, and a photographer. I take pictures of what is. I don't approve of killing anyone—not
even mice."

And now, Ruth Sellig sat in a waiting room in Greenwich Hospital reading the story of the assassin. She was
reading without being aware of what any word meant or intended, which didn't matter much because this would be
her third reading of a manuscript she did not like. She had
mastered the delicacy and intricacy of being married to
someone she loved who was a writer. Fortunately, she enjoyed most of what he had written. When he wrote something that, to her mind, was either bad writing or bad
thinking, she enjoined herself from an immediate response. "I must think about it," she would say, which

meant either an exploration of various ways of indicating that it was lousy or simply letting time pass. That was the best way; a time would usually come when he would reread it and put it to rest with, "This stinks."

But his book about assassination was something else. Sellig had linked the process of assassination to a sort of national Jungian guilt, which Ruth simply rejected; and reading the manuscript again to assess his changes was the last thing that interested her now, and with her father in the operating room, it was an untimely wifely obligation. Thus she read without reading.

Ruth Sellig adored her father. He was an internist, a family physician in this era of specialization. His wife had died many years ago of cancer, when Ruth was twelve years old, and he had never remarried, raising his child alone, treasuring her, yet using her as the reason he was unable to make a connection with another woman. When, as a student at Smith College, she fell in love with an English professor very much her senior, who had once given up his job teaching to become a naval historian in Vietnam—and become a fierce pacifist—her father was first amused and then concerned. But when they both decided to settle in Greenwich, he as a writer and she as a photographer, Seth Ferguson and Harold Sellig became fast friends. That was so many years ago, and now Dr. Seth Ferguson was in the operating room for a bypass operation that he had dismissed with a wave of his hand as, "Nothing, nothing at all."

Nellie Kadinsky, David Greene's date for the evening, was an operating-room nurse at the hospital. At age twenty-three, she was young for an OR nurse, an only child, fathered and mothered by two Polish immigrants, her father a janitor in a Stamford apartment house. At school at Tufts, she met David at an intercollegiate dance, and they had been going together for two years now,

mostly weekends and summertime. Her story of her struggle for an education and a profession put David Greene in
utter awe of her. She was a tall, rawboned young woman,
with blue eyes and straw-colored hair and almost graven
features, sometimes beautiful when she smiled, sometimes
very plain. When she was off duty, they biked together.

His competition was Dr. Harvey Loring, a very handsome divorced surgeon, whom Nellie dismissed as "no
competition at all" but nevertheless confessed a certain in-
debtedness to him for bringing her along as part of his
team.

On this night, when David picked her up at the entryway
of the hospital, her face was drawn and tired, her hair
pulled back and tied in the knot she used in the operating
room. "I've had my own day of hell," she said, "so forgive
me the way I look."

"You look good to me."

"You're a dear boy," she said, kissing him, "a very dear
boy."

"I'm a grown man of twenty-one years, ready to complete my last year of college. I don't enjoy being called a
dear boy."

"OK, you're a dear man."

"And why did you have a day of hell?" he asked as they
got into his car—and then added, "It's none of my business, is it?" He was examining his words as he spoke, having never seen her quite like this, so drawn and intense. He
had not started the car yet, a 1988 Ford Mustang.

"Where should we go?" he asked gently. "Are you hungry?"

"No." Then she added, "Forgive me, Davey. I feel rotten
and I'm being rotten."

"Oh, no. Absolutely not—I mean not rotten—I mean
maybe you feel rotten but you're not being rotten."

She turned to smile at him and kissed his cheek. "I do
love you, Davey. I spent the last hour with Dr. Ferguson's
daughter. He had a three-way bypass today, more than five

hours, and I was one of the scrubs. Do you know Dr. Ferguson?"

"Seth Ferguson? Sure. He's been our family doctor since I was born, I guess. One of an old dying breed. I hope he's all right."

"Start the car, Davey. I want to get away from here."

He nodded and turned the key. "I wanted to take you to dinner tonight, but I'm down to seven dollars and forty cents. I get paid tomorrow, but that doesn't help me tonight. We have a houseful of food at home. You want to come and pick and choose?"

"I have a pot of soup in my fridge, good soup. Soup and bread—would that satisfy you?"

"Bread and water—a loaf of bread, a jug of wine, and thou, of course—I love you, Nell, why won't you marry me?"

"Because you're dirt poor, and you don't even have a rich father. That's a mortal sin here in Greenwich."

"I have enough for a bottle of wine. And if I go to your place, can I stay over?"

"We'll see," Nellie said.

Eight

Hugh Drummond was not a sentimental man, and there were those who said he was incapable of any sentiment whatsoever, but they had never seen him with his dogs. He loved dogs passionately, British bulldogs, one of which now slept comfortably in a big leather armchair in his office. The dog's name was Churchill, and a large inscribed portrait of Mr. Churchill—the man, not the dog—hung on one of the walls of his office. On his desk were two other inscribed portraits, Ronald Reagan and George Bush. Drummond had once been Colonel Drummond, but that was in the past.

He now stood facing the big window, through which he could see the Capitol Building, gleaming in the June sunshine, his back to the two other men in the room. He always felt a quiver of personal pride when he looked through the window at the Capitol. If someone had the

temerity to ask him what was his line of work, he might
well have nodded at the big building, which would pose a
conundrum he had no desire to explain.

One of the two other men in the room, Curtis by name,
said, breaking a rather long silence, "That's a magnificent
rug. Where did you buy it?"

"Lisbon."

"I would have thought Marrakech."

"No, Lisbon."

The third man in the room held his silence, wondering
why in hell they were talking about a rug; there were more
important things to discuss. Nevertheless, the talk about
the rug turned his attention to other things in the big office,
the glass case of flintlock muskets, the huge leather-cov-
ered couch—well, Drummond was a big man, at least two
hundred and fifty pounds—and seeing the bulldog, he said
to himself, Of course, Bulldog Drummond, and then
searched his memory as to who Bulldog Drummond was.
Well, someone, he decided, and returned to the problem at
hand.

"Colonel?"

Drummond turned slowly. "You got an itch, Larry?"

"Call it that."

"What itches you?"

"Castle."

Drummond looked inquiringly at Curtis, who shrugged.
Curtis was a fat old man with white hair. He had once been
a handsome young man with blond hair, but that was all
long ago.

"Congress," Curtis said, as if that single word explained
everything.

"I am aware of that," Drummond said.

Larry spoke quietly, trying to contain his anger. You
couldn't really argue with Drummond, much less actually
get angry at him. "I'm on a very hot seat. Did you see the
Post today? Or the *New York Times*?"

"You're worried about the press conference that little
pisspot from Massachusetts held today? It's bullshit, and no

one's going to think it's anything else than bullshit. Ramoz assassinated? He walked into a speeding car, plain as day."

"The little pisspot from Massachusetts says he was pushed."

"Oh? Who pushed him?"

Larry shrugged.

"This room is not wired," Drummond said. "I made sure of that."

"Shit," said Larry, "The whole fuckin' world is wired."

"That's no way to look at things," Drummond said gently.

The fat old man, Curtis, spread his hands. "Of course it's not wired, Hugh. But Larry's not trusting. He wouldn't trust his own father." And turning to Larry, "That's a compliment, Larry," he said. "Turn on the radio, Hugh."

Larry nodded. Drummond turned on the radio. He preferred classical music and kept it tuned to WETA. The three men moved closer together and spoke softly.

"Larry, who did Ramoz?"

"Finnegan."

"Well, no one identified him. Where is he now?"

"Poor chap, he drowned."

"A sort of blessing," Curtis said. "You don't rat on the IRA and live happily ever after. But Larry, it was so long ago. The only thing anyone cares about today is Clinton and Monica. Maybe it will even satisfy some public opinion, at least those who knew about Ramoz living like a pasha down in Miami."

"This, thank God," Drummond said, "is a land with a twenty-four-hour memory. A year from now, they won't even remember Monica. I was against the killing of the nuns and the lay workers, but the goddamned Jesuits, they had to be taught a lesson, and that goes for the bishop as well. But as Curtis says, nobody remembers and nobody gives a damn. And nobody's left but the three of us."

"And Castle," Larry said. "He was with State. He put it down on paper—and those papers are still somewhere in the archives."

"Fuck Castle!" Curtis exclaimed. "He's a little shithead and he'll never open his mouth. He's an investment banker in Greenwich, Connecticut. I had dinner with him once. Lives in a big house with a new wife and he brings in two million a year. He's a happy man. Why should he do himself in?"

"I don't know why. But he knows. His signature is on soon-to-be-public documents—and to save his ass, he'll talk."

"Who was driving the car?" Drummond asked suddenly.

"I told you, Finnegan."

"Where did you get it?" Curtis demanded.

"It was Finnegan's car. That's how Finnegan drowned. He's in the car at the bottom of the bay in Florida."

"You were a congressman—and you're valuable. Don't you ever think of that, Larry?"

"All the time. That's why I'm clean."

For a minute or so, the three men were silent, while Beethoven's Third Symphony filled the room with its magnificent sound. Drummond regarded Larry thoughtfully, and finally he said, "Someday I may want you to run again, Larry, and I want to keep it with the three of us. I agree with Curtis. Castle will keep his mouth shut. If we do Castle, we have the contract man, and it begins to spread."

"I'll do it," Larry said.

"No. It's too damn dangerous—you're no mechanic!"

"Let me worry about that."

Drummond continued to stare at Larry as if he had never seen him before. Neither Larry nor Curtis spoke. Then Drummond nodded slightly, walked across the room, and clicked off the thunderous sound. "Meeting's over."

Larry excused himself for a prior engagement. He had to leave immediately. Curtis and Drummond sat in silence for a few minutes, both of them staring through the big window at the Capitol. Finally, Drummond opened a humidor on his desk and took out a cigar.

"Do you want one?" he asked Curtis.

"I'd like a shot of scotch."

Drummond went to the bar at one side of the room. It had been built as an eighteenth-century highboy, a fine reproduction and a handsome piece. He poured bourbon for himself and scotch for Curtis.

"Straight or with ice?"

"Straight."

Curtis swallowed it like water. Drummond sipped the bourbon while he cut the end of the cigar. "Curt," he said, "we're both of us older than we ever expected to be. There are just a few things in life that remain viable, and a Cuban Cohiba and good bourbon are two of them."

The British bulldog stirred.

Curtis sighed and said, "How did you ever come to pick Larry?"

"He looked like a congressman," Drummond said.

"He's a psychopath."

"Maybe. But that can be an advantage in his line of work. He started out as a sheriff in a small southern town. Killed a couple of bank robbers, and it gave him a charge. Then he shot a nigger. The man was unarmed, but snotty. Larry enjoyed it. I needed a congressman, and I picked Larry and gave him a short course in civil rights. I think he has a law degree. He's a thug, but he's obedient. Like that bulldog."

He snapped his fingers, and the bulldog waddled over to him.

Nine

David Greene bought a bottle of Italian Chianti for six dollars and seventy-five cents. Nellie warmed the soup and broke up a loaf of hot French bread, which David used to wipe up the last bit of soup in his plate. It was good soup, a mixture of beans and lentils and carrots and celery. When they had finished, with just an inch or so of wine left in the bottle, David leaned back and grinned. Nellie smiled at him.

"When you smile," David said, "you're very beautiful."

"That's nonsense. I was born gawky and I remained that way."

"I feel too good to argue, and just to see you smile is enough. You want to tell me about your rotten day?"

"If you want to hear about it?"

"Yes, I do."

She cleared the table as she spoke, the sink, stove, and

refrigerator lined up at one end of what was dining room and kitchen. The rest of the room contained a futon and a couple of chairs.

"I'll wash the dishes," David offered.

Running the hot water over the dishes, she said, "Later." She dried her hands and sprawled out on the futon. "God, I'm tired, Davey. After this summer, it's your last year, isn't it?"

"Last year. And I'll make it home every weekend."

"You're obsessed."

"Sure I am." He sprawled out on one of the two easy chairs, kicked off his shoes. "Obsessed, stricken, or whatever—I'm in love with you. Tell me about today."

"It's grisly."

"Well, that's what you do, grisly."

"Do you know what a coronary-artery bypass graft is?"

"Sort of."

"Well, it's a rather desperate way of dealing with a heart that is giving out for want of oxygen-carrying blood. This time the patient was Dr. Seth Ferguson."

David nodded. "I hope it went well."

"No, it didn't go well. It's a complex operation. The surgeon begins by removing sections of the large leg veins, and they're set aside to be used for the grafting. It takes hours, but I'll make it short. An incision is made through the breastbone, and the chest is opened, exposing the heart. Then the heart must be stopped and its temperature reduced while you switch the circulation to a heart-lung machine. I won't go into all the details, except to tell you that the leg veins are used to replace the blocked arteries, sutured, and then the heart is warmed and given a gentle electric shock to start it again. Then the chest is closed. It's a team thing and everything must be done with great precision. Harvey Loring was the surgeon, and usually he's good, but this time he botched it and excessive bleeding started—and—and I don't know. Dr. Ferguson's in intensive care now."

"Is he going to make it?"

Nellie hesitated for a long moment before she answered, "I don't know. I spent an hour with his daughter before I met you. She's very close to him. Good God, I didn't know what to tell her. If I said her father was going to make it, I'd be lying and making it worse. I don't think he's going to make it. Damn Loring! I could have done it better my-self—no, I have no right to say that."

"You like Loring, don't you?"

"No, damn it! He is likable. Everyone likes him. I don't want you to repeat this, please?"

David nodded, wondering how he would have felt had it been his father lying in intensive care, and what he would feel about a man who was responsible—yet with a part of his mind thinking that at least this was the end of Nellie and Loring as a competitive couple; and then disliking both the thought and himself as the thinker.

"Let's go to bed, Davey," Nellie said. "I want to put my arms around you and cry a little. I don't want to spend my life as a scrub nurse."

"Sure."

In bed, his arms around her, David said, "Is that real—not wanting to go on with being a scrub nurse?"

"When I feel the way I do now, it's real."

"Then what would you want to do?"

"Get married and have kids."

"Right on. I'm with you."

"David," she said woefully, "I'm three years older than you and you're at Harvard and I'm here in Greenwich, and you have a job now at Bilko's Boatyard, scraping boats for six dollars an hour, and sooner or later you'll fall in love with some pretty girl at Radcliffe or Wellesley—"

"Not likely."

"Oh, shut up and hold me."

Ten

The last of the Castle dinner guests had arrived when Richard Bush Castle was called to the phone. Castle was in the living room with his guests, and Joseph, Abel Hunt's son, was fixing drinks and passing a tray of hors d'oeuvres when Donna, the upstairs maid, informed Castle that there was a call for him in the study.

"Did he give you a name?" Castle whispered.

"No, sir. He asked for Bush."

Castle excused himself. "Only for a moment," he apologized.

Not everyone called him Bush; it was the name he had chosen for special situations—a term he loved—and for a select group of people. He explained to some, if they inquired, that it was an old family name, not connected to the family of the onetime president, but to the old Bush-Holly House. Since there was no easily available lineage of the

Bush family that had once occupied the Bush House, and since the Bush political family made no claim to a relationship with the Bush House, Castle had, so to speak, picked the name for himself unchallenged. However, Sally always called him Richard, and when she spoke of him in the third person, it was often Mr. Richard Castle or Mr. Richard. She had seen a film once where "mister" was used as a prefix by the household help and wife, and the usage had fascinated her.

The Castle household had three telephone lines, one for their son, Dickie, one for the home, and one for Mr. Castle, whose personal telephone was a tieline connected to his New York office. His home office had once been a changing room for his swimming pool, but he had rebuilt it and equipped it with his computer, printer, fax, desk, and chairs. And another extension connected to a phone in the main house, in his study.

When he picked up the phone and said, "Hello—Castle here," a voice replied, "Bush, this is Larry."

Castle had to reorient himself, and he was silent for a moment or two. He recognized the name and he recognized the voice, but it was different.

"Castle!" the voice said. "Larry."

"Yes, Congressman."

"Call me Larry."

"I just feel damn derelict, Larry. I should have called you long ago, I've been derelict." Castle was pleased with the choice of the word.

"Bush," Larry said, more gently and intimately, "you've been reading the *New York Times*?"

"Yes," Castle admitted. In his mind, Larry was coming increasingly into focus. "Yes, I have. I must say it worried me."

"Not one damn thing to worry about, Bush, not one blessed thing. But we have to talk."

"Yes. Yes, I guess we should. You're not worried?"

"Not a bit," Larry said cheerfully.

"Thank God for that. Where and when?"

"I'm in New York at the Waldorf. How about tomorrow morning, early—let's say eight A.M.—you're awake by then?"

"I'm awake, but getting into New York at that hour—"

"I'll come up to your place."

"Drive up here?" Castle hesitated.

"I'm no stranger to your home. Give me the address again and I'll find the place. You're in what they call the Back Country, aren't you?"

"That's right."

"Bush," Larry said mollifyingly, "I wouldn't put you through this bother, but I have to catch the shuttle at noon tomorrow. That squeezes me for time. I'll spend a half hour with you, and we'll put this together. It's important."

"Hey, come on, Larry. I know how important it is. As a matter of fact, I'm pleased you called, and I hope that after we talk, I can stop worrying. We have a long driveway, so I'll be at the road gate, waiting for you. Just remember that you take the Hutchinson River Parkway into the Merritt. You get off at North Street and turn left where the service road meets Lake Avenue. We're about a mile north of there."

Then Castle gave Larry the address and the off-road directions and returned to his guests. Evidently, his absence had cast no pall over the party. Muffy Platt, who had filled in for the seat of Harold Sellig's wife, was the only one who appeared bored, but her face lit up when Castle reentered the room. Mary Greene sat with Sister Pat Brody and Sally, and the monsignor was listening to a discussion between Greene and Sellig. When Castle joined them, Sally rose and announced that she had to see about dinner. It was about seven forty-five then, and Sally knew that dinner at eight was proper.

Abel Hunt considered Sally Castle to be one of the prettiest women he had ever seen, on the screen or off. As a well-educated, intelligent, race-conscious Afro-American, he knew quite well that it was his duty to denigrate the beauty of a white woman, but the innocence of Sally Castle broke through his most cherished vows. He rejected his son's notion that Sally was stupid, explaining to Joseph that in the society they both inhabited, innocence and a high degree of intelligence do not exist easily in the same individual. This evening, when Sally entered the kitchen, he greeted her with a broad smile and said, "We are ready to go. Just sit them down at the table. Cooking is an art, Mrs. Castle, and this is state of the art."

"I know. I can't fry eggs properly, so I know it better than most people."

"Someday, I will come here—no charge—and spend a day teaching you. Absolutely."

"That would be divine."

"And I gave instructions to Josie and Donna about the service. They will not screw up."

"Thank you, Mr. Hunt," Sally said, taking two bills from her bodice. "This is my own gift—something extra—a hundred for you and fifty for your son."

"Very generous of you."

"You can leave whenever you're through. As long as the girls understand the menu."

"They'll hear from me if they don't."

The two women, standing at the other side of the kitchen, giggled. Abel's son entered with a tray of glasses as Sally stood up on her toes and kissed Abel's cheek. After Sally left the kitchen, Joseph said to his father, "It's your age and beauty, so I won't mention it to Mom."

"You miss the point entirely," Abel replied. "That's a good woman, a very fine and innocent woman. I don't care why she married Castle or what she done before she married him, but that's a good, generous woman. Time you learned the difference between men and women. There are good women but mighty few good men."

"Right on!" Donna exclaimed. They were both of them, Josie and Donna, in awe of Abel.

"That's enough," Abel said firmly. "They're sitting

down. The first course and then the wine. So get your little asses in there."

Sally had spent at least an hour over the seating. She had place cards of china, small pieces that you could write a name on in ink and then simply rub it off, and the lady in the shop on Greenwich Avenue where she purchased them had assured her that they were in the best of taste. She sat at one end of the table, her husband at the other, and put Sister Pat on her right. Richard would be happy to have Muffy on his right. She knew that Castle liked to play a touching game under the table, especially with Muffy Platt, and she felt that as an understanding and grateful wife, she should overlook this. Actually, it did not bother her too much. Muffy was older and not aging well after a face-lift; and for all of his wandering, she felt that Richard would never leave her. Men were a continuing mystery to her, and thus she accepted them however they were.

Actually, the dinner party was becoming a great success, and Sally glowed. Let Richard play his game with Muffy. The old witch got little enough from her own husband, and the result would be a more amorous Richard Castle that night when they went to bed. The food was not entirely to Sally's taste—she would take off at times to stuff herself at McDonald's—but she had gotten used to odd sauces and exotic flavors; and as for the guests, they were in food's seventh heaven.

Sally herself was straining her ears, as was Sister Pat Brody, to follow a discussion between Monsignor Donovan and Harold Sellig, with an occasional intervention from Mary Greene and her husband, Herbert.

"As I understand your point of view," the monsignor was saying, "you're making a case for social guilt. In other words, it's not only the nuns and lay workers and Jesuits and Archbishop Romero who were murdered in El Salvador, presumably by assassination squads that we trained, but you include President Kennedy and Robert Kennedy and Martin Luther King—" He paused.

"And others," Sellig said. "Luminaries, of course. They provide the substance for the media. But those who die in war, of starvation, of the casual killing—"

"But that's too broad a brush," Herb Greene protested. "*Assassination* is a word of precise meaning."

"Yes, for you, Professor. You're a linguist. But in social practice, or in a literary sense, if you will, words expand and take on a broader meaning. Take two of the adjectives commonly used by the kids today, *awesome* and *cool*. Each has lost its technical meaning. Take *awesome*. My son's eighteen, going into his first year at Columbia next fall. I tell him that I've been writing the past four hours, he responds that it's positively awesome."

Sally noticed that Castle had stopped whispering to Muffy Platt and was now listening.

The monsignor was savoring his food and looking with interest at Harold Sellig, whom he had not met before.

"Would you agree, Monsignor?" Mary Greene asked. "I read Daniel Berrigan. I mean, I'm not asking whether you agree with Father Berrigan, but I think that is his point of view."

The monsignor glanced at Sellig, raising an inquiring brow.

"I never read Berrigan," Sellig said. "That's a cross I bear, an odd thing for a Jew to say, the books I should have read but never had the time to and never will, I suppose."

Smiling, the monsignor nodded. "Not so odd, Mr. Sellig. You'd be surprised to hear how many Jews I know who carry crosses—invisible ones, of course, but still very heavy."

Castle entered the conversation for the first time. "Where," he asked, "did you get your ideas about assassination, Harold?"

"Well, Richard, not out of books. I had a long lesson in Vietnam."

"Oh, please! We're not going to talk about Vietnam," Muffy said. "I am so tired of Vietnam."

"Yes, words change their meaning," Herb Greene said. "That's one of the things that make linguistics so fascinating. *Assassination* is an unusual word, derives from *hashish*. They say a group of fanatics addicted to hash murdered designated religious and political opponents by strangulation. But it is a fairly precise word. I know the Mafia has a whole vocabulary for the same process, but assassination is still political. Forgive me, I have a genetic inclination to lecture."

"It's fascinating," Sally said, and wondered why her husband frowned at her. She almost never spoke or offered any opinion when Castle's friends were there, but this comment seemed unremarkable.

The next course came and the wineglasses were topped off. Sally hadn't touched hers. She knew that a single glass of wine loosened her tongue, and she felt safer when she did not talk.

"I'm not dodging your question about Dan Berrigan," Donovan said to Mary Greene. "But you're absolutely right. He does expand the responsibility for murder and in that responsibility, he includes war. But I must add that his views on the subject are not the views of the majority of the church."

Herb Greene said, "I'm tempted to ask whether they are your views?"

The monsignor smiled. "I'm glad you're only tempted."

"Because of being married to a Catholic for some thirty years," Greene explained, "I'm frequently tempted to ask questions that shouldn't be asked."

Sellig, Jewish and married to a Presbyterian whose faith was as negative as his, said nothing, listening warily. By now the discussion had involved the entire table, and Sister Pat Brody said sharply, "I do read Dan Berrigan and his brother, Philip, and you're absolutely right, Mary. That's his point of view, and someday, God willing, it will be the whole church's point of view. And if you were to ask me, Mr. Castle"—softening her voice—"how I came to this decision, I would answer that it came out of prayer and years in places like El Salvador." She finished her glass of wine.

Sellig was relieved that his wife was not present, knowing that if she had been, she would have found some excuse to take him aside and say to him, "Harold, will you please not continue to inflict that damn book of yours on anyone and everyone who will listen." And while he was brooding over this, the monsignor confessed, "I have your manuscript on my desk. I'm trying to find time to read it."

"Do you have an extra copy of the manuscript, Harold?" Mary Greene asked, not mentioning that he had already sent her husband one, which she had given to the monsignor.

"I'm afraid I do," Sellig replied, looking somewhat confused. "In my car as a matter of fact."

Sally had never spent an evening like this. Usually, either at her dinner table or in her living room, the men talked about golf and stocks and investments and futures and other things that she was equally indifferent to, and the women spoke about the endless problems with their children and their homes and their husbands—sotto voce, although the men paid no attention to what they were talking about—and when the men engaged the women in conversation, it was limited to golf and vacation places or whispered if the man or woman was coming on—but this! This had never happened before, and she didn't really know whether she enjoyed it or found it troubling; yet while she could not understand why her husband had allowed her to invite the two clerics, she decided that she absolutely loved Sister Pat Brody, and though she was unable to make much of the conversation or what Sister Brody meant about her years in strange places, she nevertheless decided that she would go to the library one day soon and find out what or where El Salvador was and what Sister Brody had done there.

Sally was not the only person at the table mystified by Richard's willingness to include Sister Brody and Monsignor Donovan at dinner. Knowing Castle from previous occasions and plentiful gossip, both Professor Greene and his wife were surprised, though delighted, to meet such unexpected guests. Sellig was intrigued, and as for Muffy, she was, as she put it later, pissed off at their egghead chatter; but the truth was that she was interested in the monsignor, a lean, handsome, hawk-faced man who reminded her of Clint Eastwood. Her thoughts during most of the dinner, as she nibbled at the baby vegetables and the risotto, sticking to her vow of never eating more than half of any dish, were of being alone with Donovan for a few hours. A celibate man was outside of her experience, and she mused over how she might go about it.

Finally, Sally announced that there would be coffee and cognac in the living room, and that the men who wished to smoke might remain at the table. Castle had told her that this was the way "old money" did it, and while she had never encountered old money at a dinner table, she had seen the practice on film and was delighted that she could do more or less the same. Both Sellig and Professor Greene went through a shared guilt, since they were both feminists, but neither could resist the lure of valid Cohibas. Sellig salved his guilt by phoning his wife, who said to him, "I just don't know, Hal—no, I can't leave. He's still in intensive care."

"I'll join you in about an hour or less," Sellig said, assuring her that intensive care was by no means unusual in a case like this.

As Castle passed the cigars and poured brandy, he wondered what the monsignor's response would be.

"Since His Holiness has been to Cuba, I feel it mitigates a modest misdemeanor," Donovan said. "I haven't smoked a Cuban cigar in a long time. Thank you, Richard."

Eleven

Christina Manelli, the younger of Frank and Contance Manelli's two daughters, would be a sophomore at Greenwich High School after the summer break. Meanwhile, she had a job in Belle Haven as a day sitter for a family with two small children, a girl of five and a boy of seven. She worked from 10:00 A.M. to 2:00 P.M. and at times an hour or two more. She didn't mind that, and she liked the kids, and she was more than satisfied with the hundred dollars a week that they paid her. Half of it she gave to her mother, who put it into Christina's college account. Five dollars a week went to the plate at mass, which left her with forty-five dollars to spend as she wished, enough for movies and anything else she desired.

She loved to read, and one of the pleasant things about Greenwich was a book exchange that had been set up at the town dump. People brought books for which they had no use and left them at the little book shack at the dump, where volunteers put them on shelves, and they were free to anyone who wanted them.

Both Belle Haven, a corner of Greenwich shore where houses were even more expensive than in the Back Country, and the dump were within walking distance of Chickahominy, perhaps the most modest neighborhood in Greenwich; and since Christina lived in Chickahominy, she felt that her summer job was perfect.

Christina was a beautiful young woman who, living in a world of blond girls, some natural, some out of a bottle, was totally unconscious of her own beauty. She was five feet three inches, smaller than most Greenwich girls of her age, slender, with budding breasts, ivory skin, and jet black hair, cut short because she was not proud of jet black hair.

She had met Dickie Castle, Richard's son, some weeks ago at the book shack. Sally Castle, Dickie's stepmother, belonged to the Book-of-the-Month Club, the Literary Guild, and the Detective Book Club, but since Sally read only an occasional detective story, the unread books tended to pile up. Neither Dickie nor his father read books, and there were no bookshelves in the house that were not loaded with bric-a-brac—which accounted for Dickie appearing at the book shack one morning with a bag of books.

Dickie was seventeen, and he would be going into the twelfth grade at Greenwich Village School, the most pretentious, if not the most esteemed, private school in Greenwich. At seventeen, his sexual experience approached that of his father's, but that was not unusual in the circle where he moved, and perhaps because Christina was so unlike most of the girls he knew, he was taken with her. Having struck up a conversation and discovering that she appeared at the book shack between nine and ten in the morning, he managed to be there and meet her three times, each time returning books he had chosen almost at random and which he never opened.

He kept asking her for a date. Christina, ashamed to tell him that she did not date, finally gave in, got her mother's permission, and agreed to dinner and a movie. In her mind, dinner meant pizza and the movie, a local show on Railroad Avenue, where the film complex offered three choices.

Christina put on a pretty yellow cotton dress and a thin white sweater. She had no high-heel shoes, and finally she decided on her white flats instead of the sneakers she usually wore. Dickie picked her up just before six o'clock in his two-seater BMW. She had seen the BMW before, when Dickie came to the dump, but BMWs were so common in Greenwich that she didn't think it unusual that he should have one at his disposal, and she liked the style of the car with its convertible top down and black leather upholstery. She had heard her mother and father talk about the disproportion between income and car in Greenwich, so she simply accepted it, asking only, "Is it your dad's car?"

"It's mine. Dad gave it to me for my seventeenth birthday. That was almost a year ago," he added. He was a good-looking boy, blond hair and blue eyes, and if he didn't mind that she was poor, the BMW was no proof that he was rich. Of course, he went to the Village School, and that took money. But he didn't appear disturbed when he picked her up in front of the small house in Chickahominy. He didn't talk very much, except to say that he had heard that *Godzilla* wasn't a great film and that he didn't like lizards much. She asked him whether everyone called him Dickie, and he replied, "Yeah, guess so." But none of the boys she knew in high school talked very much. She said she liked Dick better, and he said, "Sure," and burst out laughing. She blushed when she realized what he was thinking.

In the movie house, he let his hand drop onto her thigh. She pushed it off. When he did it again, she said, "Please, Dickie, I'm trying to watch the film."

"It's a lousy film!" he said loudly, and heads turned in

their direction. When the movie was over, he observed, "They just try to scare you. Were you scared?"

"A little."

"It's easy to scare girls."

"Yes, I guess so." She wished they could go home and end the evening, but she didn't know how to suggest that. "We can walk to the pizza place. It's just around the corner."

"I ain't taking you to some pizza place," he said indignantly. "We're going to a real restaurant."

"Where?"

"Look, this is a date, and you're beautiful. You deserve the best. We're going to La Crémaillère. That's the best restaurant around here—trust me. I already made the reservation."

"Where is it?"

"Banksville."

She shook her head. "It's too far, Dickie. It's the other end of town."

"Twenty minutes. I open this beauty up, I can make it in fifteen."

"No, I don't want you to speed, please—" searching her mind for some way to get out of this; and at the same time, the thought intruding and telling her that none of the girls she knew had ever been to a place like La Crémaillère and what a coup that would be, and anyway, he hadn't made any moves toward her since the two attempts in the movie house. And then common sense kicked in, and she pleaded, "I have to be home by ten. I told my mom that."

"Ten! Jesus, this is a dinner date. Besides, it's only eight!"

They were already on North Street, the major north-south road in Greenwich.

"I'm not dressed for a place like that."

"You're dressed fine."

"No, please. I don't want to go there."

Dickie braked the car and slid off the road to the right,

alongside a high stone wall, one of the succession of stone walls that lined North Street, high stone walls twelve and fourteen inches thick, as if each of the expensive homes that nestled behind them was an ancient city ready to repel the barbarians.

"Look, you dumb brat!" Dickie exploded. "I'm taking you to a place where the check will be more than a hundred bucks. You'll be the first kid from Chickahominy who ever set foot in that dining room, and you're doing nothing but whining about it. What am I, chopped liver?"

Christina had never heard the expression before, and in spite of her anxiety, she began to giggle. Dickie pulled her toward him, kissed her, and fondled her breast. "Come on, come on," he begged her, sliding his hand down to her crotch. "We're going to have a great time."

She tried to pull away, shouting, "Damn you, stop! You stupid little bastard!"

"Bitch!" He slapped her with all his strength, a solid blow to her face. Her senses reeling, she managed to get the door open. Dickie grabbed her left arm and twisted. She screamed with pain, pulled loose, and stumbled out of the car into the stone wall, scratching her face.

"Get back in the car!" he yelled.

Christina curled up against the wall, her arms clutched around her, weeping with pain and frustration.

A long moment passed, and then he said, no longer shouting, "Come on, Christina. Get in the car. I'll take you home."

"Go to hell!" she burst out.

Another long moment. "All right, fuck you!" He pulled the door closed and took off like a drag racer. Christina touched her face, winced, her fingers wet with blood. When she moved her left arm, the pain was agonizing. Curled up like that, she was like another big rock or a pile of something, anything, in the lights of the occasional car that passed. It was just past twilight, and darkening quickly. Bad luck breaks sooner or later, and this time it was Abel Hunt and his son, driving home from the Castles'.

Abel's eyes were on the road, and to his peripheral vision, the splash of the yellow dress might have been an early cluster of daylilies, briefly illuminated in the darkness, but his son cried out, "Pop, stop! Stop!" The car screeched to a halt. "Back up." It was dark now, and the road was empty. "Pop, pull over on the shoulder."

They both got out of the car and walked to Christina, still curled up in a protective ball.

"My God," Joe said, "it's Christina."

Abel bent over her. "Christie—Christie."

She looked up at the big black man, looming over her and shrank back.

"Christie, it's Abel Hunt."

Recognition dawned, and Christina began to weep. Abel bent over and gently raised her to her feet. "Can you walk?"

She nodded.

Abel wiped the mixture of blood and tears from her face. She tried to say something but her voice failed.

"Don't try to talk now, honey. Let me get you into the car and we'll take you home." Abel put her in the front seat, next to him, strapped on the seat belt, and drove on to Chickahominy. By the time they parked in front of the Manelli house, Abel had most of the story, and he said to Christina, "Joe and I are going in with you. That's best because Frank is going to blow his top. I know Frank."

"Please, do I have to tell them?"

"No other way, Christie. You're hurt, and they have to know why. I'd like to kill that little bastard, but I'm not Frank and I react differently."

"Dad will kill him."

"That's why we're going in with you."

"It's my fault."

"No, it's not your fault, and don't get off on that track." He rang the doorbell, placing himself in front of Christina.

Joe stood beside him, whispering, "Should I sit in the car?"

"Stay with me," Abel said.

Joe put his sweater over Christina's shoulders. She was shivering, in spite of the warmth of the evening. Connie Manelli opened the door and, not immediately aware of Christina, blocked by Abel's huge bulk, greeted them with a smile. "Abel, what a surprise."

"Now take it easy, Connie. I got Christina here—she's all right. Bruised, but all right, so don't scream or shout."

He stepped aside, and Connie saw Christina, dropped her jaw, and then folded her weeping daughter into her arms.

From inside the house, Frank's voice, "Connie, what's going on out there?"

Abel walked into the house and into the kitchen. Frank and his wife had been playing rummy, and the cards were spread out on the kitchen table. In another room, the television was on.

"Abel," Frank said, "what's up?" And then, hearing sounds, "What the hell's going on out there?"

"Now you just take it easy," Abel said, blocking Frank's movement toward the front door. "Christie's with me. She's hurt a bit, but all right. I want you to take it easy."

Now Constance entered the kitchen with Christina, and Joe behind them.

"Hello, Daddy," Christina managed to say. "I'm all right. Please don't get angry."

"What happened? Tell me what happened."

"Sit down!" Abel said firmly. "Sit down and I'll tell you what happened. Connie, take her into the bathroom."

"Will someone tell me what the hell is going on!"

"Take her into the bathroom, Connie. You sit there," he told Frank, "and listen to me. She had a date with Dickie Castle."

"What! Dickie Castle! I'll kill that little son of a bitch!"

Frank Junior and Dorothy came into the kitchen to see what the shouting was about, and Frank yelled, "Get out of here, both of you. Go watch television, and stay out of here."

"Now listen, Frank," Abel said firmly. "Joe and me, we were driving back from Castle's place, and we saw Christie by the road. We picked her up and brought her home. Her story is that she had a date with Dickie. He took her to a movie and made some moves, but she brushed him off. Then he told her he was taking her to dinner at La Crémaillère, and he made some more moves and she said, Take me home, and a struggle started and she got out of the car and fell against one of those high stone walls and cut her face. Maybe her arm is broken or dislocated. Anyway, it's painful and you'd better take her to the hospital."

Through his teeth, Frank whispered, "Did he rape her?"

"No! And I mean no!"

"I swear to God I'll kill that little bastard!" He got out of the chair. "I'm going out there and I'm going to beat that little bastard until—"

Pushing him back into the chair, Abel said, "You are not, or you'll have to do it over my dead body. You'll talk to that poor kid and then you'll take her to the hospital. And I'm going with you because I love you and thank God I don't have an Italian temper. After that, we go to the cops, both of us—or do I have to tie you to this chair? Jesus God, this is nothing. He didn't rape her, and she learned something. But if you beat up that boy or kill him, your life's over. What do your kids do then? What does Connie do? What does Christie do? You touch that boy, and you got a lawsuit you'll be paying for the rest of your life. Now, are you going to act sane or not?"

Frank nodded.

"Give her a few hugs and a kiss, and then we'll take her to the hospital—agreed?"

Frank nodded again, and Abel said to Joe, "Drive home, Joey, and tell Mom what I'm into, not to worry. And tell her not to talk about it, and you keep your mouth shut, too. I don't want this all over the neighborhood."

Twelve

Muffy was the first to leave the dinner party at the Castles'. Richard Castle took her to the door, asking her to stay a bit longer, being that it was only nine-thirty, to which she replied, "Richard, did you really expect me to sit there with that old schoolteacher and that fat nun? What could I say to them, except that it must be a great pleasure to be a nun and eat yourself silly. No, thank you."

"How long will your husband be away?"

"God knows. He's buying or selling something in Brazil or Switzerland."

"Then let's get together sometime. Lunch in New York—maybe my place at the Carlyle. We could eat in the room, and who knows what else?"

"Call me." She lit a cigarette as she spoke, puffed, and smiled at it, satisfied. "I've been dying for one, and by the way, that cigar-at-the-table notion of yours is way out. Not done, Richard, except in British films."

"Those Cuban Cohibas cost me over twenty-five dollars a shot."

"Call me, Richard."

In the living room, the stout nun and Mary Greene did have something to say to each other, and in contrast to Muffy, Sally was an appreciative audience. "I do like Harold and I love his wife, Ruth," Mary said, "but I am more than confused by his ideas about assassination. I've read everything else of his, and they were all run-of-the-mill best-sellers. You know, he sent a copy of his manuscript to Herb, but I haven't gotten to it. This notion of collective guilt—may I ask you what you really think of it, Pat?"

Pat shook her head. "I just don't know. A number of Catholic writers have speculated about it, and of course both the Berrigan brothers have edged toward it."

"It's a terrible thought. Back in December of 1984, there was an explosion at the Union Carbide plant in India, and eight—I don't know now, maybe twelve—thousand people died. The release of some deadly gas killed all those people."

"I remember it," Sister Brody said. "We prayed for them."

"We owned some Union Carbide stock, just a hundred shares, and we sold it immediately. And there was a night, a few days later," Mary went on, "after a day of Christmas shopping, that I lay awake all night thinking of that awful thing and the shares of Union Carbide stock we had owned, and I went to mass that morning and then I had to face the kids in school—I had a class of eight-year-olds that semester, and I looked at their bright clean faces— well, it took me time to get over it, and then tonight."

Sally listened and wondered why she knew nothing about this. She was living on the West Coast in 1984, with a previous husband. There was a whole world she had never ventured into.

"Didn't you talk to anyone?" Sister Brody asked.

"I talked to Herb. He said I was overemotional. I remember him bringing up the subject of the Holocaust. His argument was that there was no such thing as collective guilt, and that owning shares in a company, any company, did not make one responsible for the company's actions."

"I can understand that," Pat agreed. "We have taken gifts from companies whose practices are deplorable."

"But truly, what do you think?"

"Truly? Well, truly, I don't know what I think. I take refuge in prayer."

Sally, speaking for the first time, recalling that before they were married, Richard had been an Assistant Secretary of State for Central America, asked, "Could you tell me what happened in El Salvador? I'm so ignorant—I don't even know where it is or what it is."

Both women were taken aback by the simple innocence of the question, and Mary Greene realized that no other woman she knew would ask a question like that. Sister Brody responded to it without noticeable hesitation:

"El Salvador is a tiny country in Central America. Back between 1979 and 1992 there was a struggle of the poor farmers, who had no land to speak of, against the large landholders, who owned almost all of the good land and ruled with terror. I was there then, for several years. I am ashamed to say that our government armed and trained so-called death squads, murder squads if you ask me, to enforce the large landowner's rule with terror. These murder squads raped and killed a group of nuns and lay workers, and then murdered a Catholic bishop on the altar and six Jesuit priests. They killed over 70,000 other good people, but the murder of the nuns and priests made more headlines."

"This really happened?" Sally asked.

"Yes, my dear. It really happened."

"But why the nuns and the priests?"

"Because we worked with the poor, because we gave them food and established schools and taught them sanitation."

"But we're a good country," Sally pleaded. "We don't do things like that."

Meanwhile, at the dinner table, the Cuban Cohibas had been smoked and the brandy sipped, and Sellig remembered that he had promised to join his wife at her hospital vigil and Professor Greene, increasingly guilty at this separation of the sexes, said that he, too, had to go and be up early the following morning. Castle did not object to an early end for the evening, but he said to Monsignor Donovan that he would like a few words with him alone. The Greenes and Sellig took their departures, and both Sister Brody and Sally appeared satisfied to spend another half hour in the living room.

Sally couldn't imagine what her husband might want with Monsignor Donovan, but since both asked for the favor of a conversation alone with goodwill and without rancor, she was reassured and delighted by the opportunity to talk more with Sister Brody.

Castle suggested that he and Donovan retire to his study, where they would be more comfortable. He was proud of his study, which had been decorated by Maxine Dibble, recommended to him by George Lark, president of the North American Industrial Bank. He made a point of this to certain acquaintances, but decided that he would not mention it to the monsignor. Anyway, the study spoke for itself. On one wall were four Audubon prints, which he had purchased at auction when Mayor Koch decided to sell an original Audubon folio discovered in the basement of the New-York Historical Society. On another wall were a Renoir painting and a bookcase with shelves of books, leather bound, with classic titles, but which were not books at all but backings to cover a large safe. This, too, he refrained from mentioning. A bay window looked out on the garden, which the monsignor had been led through earlier in the day, and on the floor was an Aubusson rug, a very good copy of the original in the Mount Vernon home of George Washington. The walls were paneled in mahogany, and the room was furnished with an antique partners desk, a leather sofa, and three overstuffed chairs.

Castle was pleased that Donovan admired the room, and he asked the monsignor to sit down and offered another humidor of Cohiba cigars.

"Oh, no." Donovan shook his head. "How on earth do you get them? No, I shouldn't ask that."

"No secret, Monsignor. They're sent to me from Washington. A congressman there—I won't mention his name, of course—has an arrangement with one of the embassies in Washington."

The monsignor nodded. He was beginning to feel uneasy but decided that, considering the circumstances that brought him here and considering a dinner menu such as he rarely experienced, he could not object to a talk with this man.

Castle apologized for lighting another cigar. "I talk better while I'm smoking, and this is the only place, except the dining room and my office, that I foul up. I turned half of the pool house into an office. I have an office in New York, but I can work just as well from here. I'm a very rich man, Monsignor, and I'd like to give you a check for your church for listening to my prattle."

He appeared entirely unaware of the maladroitness of his offer, and the monsignor, taking it as a matter of course in Castle's milieu, was highly tempted to accept. Heaven knows, his church needed the money, but he had to refuse and remind Castle that as a guest he could not accept it.

"I don't know one damn thing about any religion," Castle said. "My parents were Baptists, but we were too damn poor to have a car and get to church. That was another life. I was poor, now I'm a rich investment banker. I'm talking out of turn, but I have to talk, and I feel that I'm talking to you in confidence. I heard that you can talk to a Catholic priest in total confidence?"

Donovan nodded. "Yes, if one is a Catholic and undertakes what we call confession. But you're not Catholic, Mr. Castle, and while I can assure you that anything you say to me is confidential, I cannot say that it's privileged—I mean in a legal sense."

"I understand. I'm not religious, and when we moved here to Greenwich, I joined Christ Church—the big one on the Post Road next to the Jewish temple—because that's where the people I knew belonged. I hate to say this and I don't mean it as any put-down of religion, but that's the way I am. I joined the Hill Crest Club because my friends belonged to it. It didn't matter to me that it was an Episcopal church, I mean Christ Church. I give them five thousand a year and I turn up with Sally and my son at Christmastime and Easter."

Donovan realized that there had to be a point to all this and he wondered where it was leading. He knew how unusual it was for a man in Castle's position to talk like this, and he decided that the easiest answer to his question was to ask. "You want help, Mr. Castle. That appears obvious, if I may say so. What can I do for you?"

"Well, it's a matter of public record, so it's not a question of privileged information. During the Bush administration I was one of the Assistant Secretaries of State. My field was Central America."

"I still don't fully understand. Are you referring to the dinner-table conversation?"

"Sort of. I mean the business in El Salvador."

"Were you concerned in that?"

"That's just the trouble. I got you in here with the feeling that I could talk to you in a way that would be privileged. Then you tell me that's not the case. Now I don't know what to say."

The man had his hand out, and Donovan did not know what to put in it. There were so many bits and pieces mixed up in their conversation that the monsignor could not think of any way to sort them out: religion, guilt, murder possibly, or perhaps something less than murder that he could not grasp. Donovan had in his pocket sixteen dollars and change that had to last to his next paycheck. He was a man who had lived for years attempting not to be judgmental, and he was being asked for help by a man so far apart from him on the economic scale that there was almost no possible meeting ground; yet he lived by the belief that there was always a meeting ground.

"I can't allow you to tell me things in the manner of a confession. Do you believe in God, Mr. Castle?"

"What?"

Why such surprise? Donovan wondered. After all, he had sought out a priest to talk to, or perhaps not sought him out, but he had grasped the opportunity to talk when his wife brought one here.

"I asked you whether you believed in God. That's not such an unusual question for a priest to ask, very personal perhaps, but you did indicate to me that this was a very personal conversation."

Castle nodded but did not speak, and as the silence extended, the priest repeated the question, "Do you believe in God?"

Forced to enter himself and examine himself, Richard Castle spoke very slowly. "The truth is, I never much thought about it." Pause again. "That's a hell of a thing to say, isn't it? Nobody ever asked me that before."

"Never?"

"No, I don't think so."

"Don't you regard that as a bit strange?"

An introspective exchange was something rare in Castle's world. At this point he felt a sense of futility, but he was also unable to end the dialogue, partially because he did not want to surrender it. He wanted answers to questions he could not bring himself to ask.

"No, I don't think so, Monsignor. I grew up as a poor kid in the South. I suppose I took it for granted that a preacher talked about God, not anyone else. I lived with all sorts of people, and I lived different lives. I worked my way through college to a degree in business administration. I went to Washington and worked my way through law school. I'm sixty-three years old, and I got a lot of polish on the way up. But nobody ever asked me whether I believed in God. I mean on Wall Street"—he smiled slightly—"well, maybe some pray for the market to go up—but God . . . I'm trying to say something—I mean, you die. What happens then? I don't know whether this makes any sense at all to you, but the only thing I ever thought seriously about was being rich. Now I'm rich enough. But God? You don't ask that—nobody does."

"I asked you."

"You did. I'll have to think about it."

"I'd also like to know what conclusion you come to, and when you come to it, whatever it is, I'd like to know. Perhaps we can talk again. You can find me at St. Matthew's. It's getting late now, and I'm afraid Sister Brody and I must go."

"One more thing. I wouldn't say this to anyone else in the world, and maybe it's because I'm sixty-three, and every time my heart skips a beat, I think that this is it. I'm not much damn good. I think I love my wife, but tonight, when my friend Muffy was leaving, I tried to make a date to see her in New York—"

Donovan interrupted him: "No, Mr. Castle! I can't have you confessing to me."

Castle's smile was unexpected. "You're right. You know what Groucho Marx said, 'I wouldn't join a club that would have me as a member.' "

"I don't mean it that way," the monsignor said softly.

"No, of course not. Do me one favor, let me write out a check for your church."

Donovan looked at him searchingly. "Why?"

Castle shrugged. "I feel I'm in deep shit up to my neck. Something happened to me tonight. I never talked like this before. I dumped on you; I don't dump on people. On Wall Street, I'm one crafty, nasty son of a bitch. That's what I am and I'm no damn different now, but I'm tired. I'm just so fuckin' tired."

"Will it help if you write me a check?"

"Yes."

"All right. I'd like to help. Make it out to St. Matthew's Church."

Castle went to his desk, took out a checkbook, and wrote the check. He handed it to the monsignor.

"This is for ten thousand dollars," Donovan said.

"I won't miss it."

"Thank you."

"For Christ's sake, don't thank me."

"I must, Castle. It will do a lot of good."

"I've spent a lifetime hating do-gooders. I still do. I haven't changed."

The monsignor and Sister Brody left. Sister Brody kissed Sally and said she would see her again. The monsignor thanked Castle for a good evening. When he and the nun were in the car, driving back to the neighborhood where their church was located, Sister Brody said, "I suppose you have no intention of telling me what went on between you and Castle?"

"That's an excellent supposition."

"I have the right to be curious, considering what I've heard about the man."

"Everyone has the right to be curious. We can thank God for that." Then, after a moment, he added, "Castle gave me a check, made out to St. Matthew's, for ten thousand dollars."

"What! I don't believe you."

"Sister, Sister."

"Ten thousand dollars—that's wonderful."

"I argued against it. I didn't want to take it."

"You argued against it? For heaven's sake, do you know how much we need that money, how much we can do with it, how many hungry mouths can be fed, how much food and medicine we can send to El Salvador and Guatemala—"

"Sister, please don't lecture me! I happen to know exactly what we can do with it."

Thirteen

Harold Sellig drove away from the dinner party to join his wife at the hospital. He was full of good food, two glasses of wine, the lingering taste of the Cuban cigar, and a heavy load of guilt. He felt that he should have been with his wife at the hospital, that she was facing perhaps the most serious crisis of her life and that he had allowed her to go and keep a vigil alone because he selfishly desired to make a clinical study of a very rich man and his trophy wife. He had gone with her urging and with Dr. Ferguson's assurance that the operation was a "lead-pipe cinch." Harold said he had no idea of what a lead-pipe cinch was, and Dr. Ferguson had carefully explained that in ancient times—some fifty or sixty years ago—underground utility connections were sealed with hot lead. Harold had grown up with a father who never understood him, and when he married Ruth, Dr. Ferguson had adopted him as the son he never had.

On board the aircraft carrier, off the coast of Vietnam and amid the screeching, banging hellish noise of an aircraft carrier in action, Harold, as a naval historian, found solace in the antique game of pinochle, which he played with two sailors from the engine room, who taught him the game. He brought the game home with him, and some of the best hours of their marriage were spent with Dr. Ferguson, playing pinochle, a game that can only be played with grim seriousness and loving anger.

He and Ruth had frequently argued about and discussed "Jewish guilt." She held that it was genetic, but Dr. Ferguson rejected that view and said there was a limit to how much you could blame on the genes. He put it to the series of misfortunes that spelled out Jewish history, but Ruth insisted that the whole idea of the victim carrying the burden of guilt was fallacious. Harold dutifully excised from his speech any mention of guilt; nevertheless on occasions such as this, he wallowed in it.

It was a half hour past ten when he reached the hospital, parked, and went to the waiting room, where he found Ruth, drawn and tired, talking to a young redheaded man, who was introduced to him as David Greene.

"You're Herb's son?"

David nodded.

"How's it going with Seth?" Harold asked Ruth.

"Not good," she said bleakly.

Harold put his arms around her and kissed her. She tightened the embrace and clung to him. That spelled out her condition to her husband. She was not a clinging woman.

"What happened?"

"Dad's back in the operating room."

"Why? What happened?"

"I don't know what happened. But they called the surgeon back and Dad's in the operating room again."

"Now?"

"Yes, now."

Harold turned to look at David.

"I don't know much more than that, Mr. Sellig. I was with my girlfriend, Nellie Kadinsky, when Dr. Loring called her and told her to meet him here, at the hospital. She's his scrub nurse, and he said it was an emergency. I drove her here, and I'm waiting for her." David hesitated, not knowing what else he should say. He felt he had no right to pass on Nellie's comments about the operation, and he knew it would only make things worse for Ruth Sellig.

"What kind of an emergency? Did she say?"

David shook his head. "I don't know."

Harold drew Ruth over to a couch, and she huddled against him. He knew enough about bypass operations to realize that stopping the heart twice in a matter of hours was no small thing. What would Seth Ferguson's death do to Ruth? Her relationship with her father was, he felt, stronger than their own relationship. When she whispered, "Hal, what will I do if he dies?" and he assured her that Seth would not die, it was like the cold wind of death flowing over both of them. He hated hospitals. He had spent hours in the ship's hospital of the carrier. Terrible things happen on an aircraft carrier, things that the public is never informed of. Every landing of a plane was a passage with death, and Harold remembered a visit to the bomb hold, where there was enough explosive to blow away an entire country; and there the stink of death was not a smell but a vibration thick as molasses, and that was the way it felt in this waiting room now.

He simply could not ask Ruth whether she had read any of the manuscript or the changes he had made in it. That would be like asking her whether she had touched base with death.

"How long since the surgeon was here?" he asked. "Did you see him?"

"For a moment."

"Did he say anything?"

"Just that there were complications and that he had to hurry off."

There was nothing to say that Harold could think of, and Ruth was silent, her mind filled with memories of fishing in the Long Island Sound when she was a small girl, when she was eleven and twelve, the two years after her mother had died of cancer. They kept a small rowboat at Tod's Point, that strange finger of land that Greenwich was so proud of, and they would go bottom fishing with no poles, just string lines, and occasionally they would hook a flounder or blowfish, throw back the blowfish and take the flounders home. Those were wonderful days, and sometimes they would just sit and drift with the incoming tide, and she would read to Seth, while he smoked his pipe and allowed the delicious smell to drift past her.

Those are death thoughts, she told herself with annoyance, and said to Harold, "He'll make it, won't he? Tell me that he'll make it."

"Of course, he'll make it."

It was more than an hour since Harold had come there, and as they spoke, Seth Ferguson was already dead, and Dr. Loring was firming up his resolve to go to the waiting room and inform Ruth that her father had passed away.

He entered the waiting room, still in his green gown, and stood looking at David and Harold and Ruth. Then he walked over to Ruth.

"I'm so sorry. We tried everything we could. His heart was too weak. I'm sorry."

Fourteen

While Harold and Ruth Sellig and David Greene were waiting to hear the results of Dr. Ferguson's second operation, Frank Manelli and Abel Hunt were in the emergency room, on the ground floor where Christina had been taken to have her arm x-rayed.

They were alone in the small waiting room. The emergency room at the hospital was not a very busy place at this hour, and they had a bit of time to talk without Christina's presence. Manelli was still pushing to go on out to the Castles' place, and Abel was still trying to cool him off.

"Like I said," Abel told him, "you stay out of this. What are you after? Revenge? This is a part of a kid's growing up. She learned something about people. Lessons are painful but necessary."

"I don't buy that."

"If you want revenge, sue him."

"I don't sue people. You know what it costs to sue someone?"

"We'll go to the cops," Abel assured him. "That's punishment enough. They'll go out to Castle's place and arrest the kid, and Castle will have to post bond. The kid will have a record."

"He probably has a record already. I'm pissed off. I want to put my hands on that little bastard."

"Good. Then you'll be arrested, too."

The arrival of a young intern with Christina and the X rays put an end to their conversation. "Nothing broken or dislocated," the intern told them cheerfully. "She has a sprained shoulder, and we'll give her a sling. I'll give you a couple of patches to change the ones I put on her face. Just scratches. She'll be fine. Some swelling around the arm, nothing else. She's very beautiful. The scratches won't leave any scars, so she'll be just as beautiful."

Christina squirmed with the praise. As with any fifteen-year-old, the sling was a sort of status symbol. She had already decided to say nothing to anyone about what had happened. The sling would add to the mystery.

From the hospital, they drove to the police station, down Mason Street almost to the Sound. There is a ridge that runs for miles along the Connecticut coast, at times near the Long Island Sound, at times a mile or two away from it. The business section of Greenwich, where the police station is located, is down from the ridge and closer to the Sound, just a few minutes drive from the hospital at that time of the night.

While Greenwich is considered one of the wealthiest towns in America, to New York City what Beverly Hills is to Los Angeles, it is far larger than Beverly Hills, sixty thousand people, running the gamut from the outrageously rich to the middle class and then to the poor—which gives its police a peculiar problem—ultrarich neighborhoods where they have to tread very carefully. If you think of cops in terms of tarnish, they are by no means untarnished.

Sergeant Yeats was at the desk, and after he listened to

Frank and studied the two angry men and the sad-faced girl thoughtfully, he asked her, "How do you feel now, Christina?"

"It hurts. In more ways than one."

"You state that you were not raped. Was there any attempt at rape?"

"He came on to me . . ." She hesitated. "I think he wanted to."

"How do you feel about letting this pass?"

"No way!" Frank exclaimed.

"Has the kid ever been charged?" Abel asked.

"Yes, he's been in trouble. But I'm asking your daughter," he said to Frank.

"Whatever my dad says," Christina replied.

"You want him arrested, Mr. Manelli?"

"Damn right."

"OK. I'll send a couple of officers out there, and they'll bring him in. I have to tell you that the old man is a decent guy. He supports our Silver Shield drive generously. I'm not trying to make an exception; we get a good deal of this here in town, and generally it's simply a fine—as long as the parent cooperates and makes the kid work for it."

"As long as you arrest him and put the fear of God into him."

At this point Frank had cooled down considerably, and they left the station house and drove back to Chickahominy, dropping Abel off at his house.

Abel's wife, Delia, his son, Joe, and his two daughters, Sarah and Helen, were still up, sitting at the kitchen table and waiting for him. Delia had coffee ready, and there was raisin pound cake on the table.

"How about some ham and eggs?" Abel said. "Sunnyside up. How about that, Delia, my own sweet love?"

"You mean you didn't eat at the party?"

"I am starved." And turning to his kids, he said, "How about you all get upstairs to bed. Gossip, gossip. You'd all sell your britches for a little juicy gossip."

"I don't wear britches," Sarah said.

"And we just wanted to hear how Christie is. See?"

"Christie's just fine." Delia was already setting up the pan and preparing to slice ham. "You know, Honeybunch," Abel said, "that I don't eat at a party. I can't eat when I'm doing the cooking. I taste. And you're letting the pan get too hot."

"Just don't teach me how to cook," Delia said.

"No way, never," Abel agreed.

Fifteen

Nellie, changed into her street clothes, went to the room where David was waiting for her. Harold and Ruth were still there, Ruth crying and Harold with his arm around her. Nellie went to them and asked whether she could help. Rising, Harold took her aside.

"My wife would like to see him, her father."

"Yes, I can understand that. They took him into the pathology room, and she can see him if she feels strongly about it." Nellie spoke in a whisper. "But it wouldn't be good now. Tomorrow, after the undertaker removes the body—well, Dr. Ferguson will look better."

"What undertaker?" He had no idea how one went about a burial.

"Dr. Ferguson was a Protestant?"

"Yes—if he was anything. He left instructions to be cremated, I believe."

"Protestants usually use Halley, I mean if you do it here in Greenwich. That's—" She spelled it out, and Harold jotted it down. "You don't have to do anything tonight. I have a couple of sleeping pills here. Try to get her to take them. In the morning, you can call Mr. Halley, and he'll call the hospital and pick up the body." She gave him a small bottle with two yellow pills in it. "She can take both of them. Mr. Halley will tell you exactly what to do, and when you can both go over there and look at the body. But take your wife home now, if you can talk her out of going to the pathology room."

Harold told Ruth what Nellie had said, and she agreed; he helped her rise. His manuscript was stuffed into the large purse she carried, and he wondered briefly whether she had even looked at it.

When they had left, Nellie turned to David. "You poor kid. I plucked you out of bed in the middle of good lovemaking, and now you've been sitting here for hours."

"It's all right. She had someone to talk to."

"You didn't mention anything I said to you—about him having flubbed it?"

"Goodness, no."

"Thank God. There was some bleeding internally, but that didn't do it. His heart stopped, and we couldn't start it again. There was just too much damage. Dr. Loring is sitting in his office now, getting drunk and still in his operating clothes—and, David," she said, taking a deep breath, "I'll marry you."

"What? What on earth!"

"If you'll have me?"

He threw his arms around her and kissed her. "Will I have you? Will I ever! But what—?"

"Death. It's as simple as that." She clung to him.

Sixteen

Harold drove Ruth home. Sitting beside him, Ruth managed to say, "Don't talk to me, Hal. I just want to be inside of myself and remember."

"Inside of myself and remember" lodged in Harold's mind, and he looked at his wife as if he had never seen her before. Just as he had been the son Seth Ferguson never had, Seth Ferguson was the father he never had. His father, his own father, had a savage distaste for everything he did, writing, joining the navy, becoming a part of the Vietnam tragedy, his rejection of religion, his contempt for wealth, and in all these things he had found a soul mate in Seth Ferguson. He was not a weeping person and he found it almost impossible to cry; yet now his eyes welled with tears and he wished in his heart that Seth Ferguson still existed somewhere. He remembered one of the many conversations with Seth, when Seth had mentioned that he didn't want to be put in any damn coffin and be food for the worms. "And I don't want any of this nonsense about an afterlife. God Almighty, the sheer boredom of it!" How strange that he had used that expression! "Just incinerate me, and don't keep the ashes." That was the word he had used, *incinerate.*

Yet there had been one conversation where Seth had backed off and said to Harold, "I must admit, Hal, that one thing keeps me from being a card-carrying member of the atheists' society—and that's the damn human liver. The more I study it, the more I'm confounded. It defies every process of evolution and natural selection. Do you realize that the liver performs over five hundred functions that we know about and more that we haven't discovered yet. Liver tissue consists of thousands of tiny lobules, and these are constructed of hepatic cells, and these are the basic metabolic cells. The liver function involves the digestive system, excretion, detoxification, blood chemistry. It produces bile for the process of fat digestion, it stores glucose—and God only knows what else it does, and I could sit here all evening listing other functions that we have already discovered, and there's just no way, absolutely no way, that I can conceive of this as a result of natural selection."

"What then?" Harold had asked.

"Damned if I know! I sat for an evening listening to Carruthers, the best liver man in the country, and when I put it to him, he brushed it off and said, Don't get into this God business. It's too confusing."

Harold was not too concerned with fate or faith or his past, and he had lost his last shred of faith—if he ever had any—when he was ashore in Vietnam right in the middle of the Tet offensive. Like many others who had been in Vietnam, he was terrified of his dreams, and each night when he went to bed, he instructed his mind not to dream. Sometimes it worked, mostly it did not.

The manuscript, now stuffed into Ruth's purse, had come in large part out of the Vietnam experience and out of his talks with Seth Ferguson, and while Seth lay dying and

Ruth sat her lonely vigil in the waiting room, he had been at the Castles', stuffing himself with rich food. They were home now and in the garage. He turned off the motor, dropped his head against the wheel, and began to cry like a child, sobs that wracked his entire body.

"Baby, baby," Ruth said. "It's all right. Baby, don't."

Things had been reversed.

Seventeen

Hugh Drummond met Larry in his room at the Waldorf. Larry had checked in a few hours before and had made himself comfortable in a spacious room, large enough to accommodate a couch and a couple of easy chairs. He had a bottle of bourbon and a bucket of ice ready, and he poured half a tumbler of the whiskey for Drummond.

"I don't have too much time," Drummond said. "I'm on a midnight flight, destination Bermuda."

"Bermuda?"

"They're sending out subpoenas tomorrow. Curtis says I'm not on the list, but I need a vacation—and they can't serve a subpoena in Bermuda."

"That stinks. How do you know?"

Drummond took a full swallow of the bourbon, licked his lips, took out a cigar, cut the end, and lit it. "Curtis finds out such things." He knew the question that was on Larry's tongue.

"Will they subpoena me?"

"No, according to Curtis." Drummond smiled. "But they will subpoena Castle."

"I don't have a gun," Larry said. "Curtis told me to meet you here. You told him you would take care of it."

"Of course. You know, Larry"—blowing a ring of smoke—"Curtis is an extraordinary man. He's eighty-two years old."

"No. You're kidding."

"Scout's honor, eighty-two, and he has a mind like a steel trap. All these years I've been telling you to keep clean—well, it's paid off. When I come back and all this has blown over, you can be a congressman again, if that's what you want."

"I have a source here in New York—for the gun, I mean—but he knows me."

"You don't need it," Drummond said. "Clean is clean." He reached into his jacket pocket and took out a gun and a silencer. "I have my own source, a few things I keep in a small apartment here. Clean is clean, Larry. This is a thirty-eight automatic with a silencer, a new gun." He was wiping it as he spoke. "Be sure it's a head shot—no mistakes. I presume you'll rent a car?"

"Yes. But I need ID."

"You do indeed." Again, he took a moment to blow a ring of smoke. "I used to do that for my grandsons, Larry. They loved it. Nothing I did fascinated them as much. About the ID." He reached into his breast pocket and took out two cards, which he handed to Larry. "Driver's license and American Express. Curtis obtained them. They were stolen from the home of a CIA man who is in Mexico with another set of IDs. So there will be no notification that they were stolen until next week, when he returns. If you're curious, the young man who stole them is having an affair with the CIA man's wife. He sold them to Curtis for five hundred dollars. Money will buy anything, if you know where to look for it. I would impress on you that you should have no other identification on your person. Use the American Express card, and then destroy both the card and the license. Leave your wallet in the hotel safe."

"Well, I'll be damned," Larry said. "Some kid fucking a CIA man's wife. You can't trust anyone."

"That's a thought, Larry." Drummond permitted himself another smile.

"How long will you be in Bermuda?"

"I have no idea, Larry. Talk to Curtis if you want to reach me. I have some other plans, but this isn't the time to talk about them."

Eighteen

After the monsignor and Sister Brody had departed, Sally asked Richard, somewhat tentatively, whether he had enjoyed the evening. She had no idea what his response would be and no idea of what had passed between him and the monsignor.

Looking at her rather strangely, as if her question was totally unexpected, he didn't answer immediately. She imagined she had offended him by inviting the priest and the nun, but she didn't understand why, if their presence was offensive, he had not put his foot down when she first asked whether she could invite them.

Finally, he said, "*Enjoy* isn't the right word. I liked the priest, but I didn't get a chance to talk to the nun. You spoke to her. Did you like her?"

Sally nodded. He almost never asked her opinion about anything.

"She was very kind."

"Kind?" His brow knit. "Why do you say kind?"

"She helped me," Sally said without conviction.

"For God's sake, Sally, you're afraid of me. I haven't been that bad to you, have I?"

"No, of course not. You've been very good to me. No one was ever so good to me."

"Then tell me how she helped you," he said, softening his voice.

"Well—I mean"—struggling for the words—"about myself—about what makes me unhappy."

He had never felt that she was unhappy. She was always smiling and always being very sweet to anyone who came by and never angry at what anyone did. In Richard's mind, notwithstanding that she would be forty in a month or two, she was the most beautiful woman he had ever known, and in bed she responded lovingly to whatever measure or aspect of sex he had in mind.

"But you're not unhappy," he protested. "I know I'm more than twenty years older than you, but before you married me you said that makes absolutely no difference. I know you had terrible difficulties in your childhood. Does it make you unhappy because I keep telling you what to do?"

Actually, she was grateful for that. When she brought home a dress that Richard didn't like, she exchanged it. When he mentioned her table manners, she immediately corrected them to do as he said. She knew Richard was very smart, that he had a college degree and a law degree, and she willingly accepted the fact that he knew about everything—how she should dress, how to greet people, the names of the flowers in the garden—and when they went to the club, he always chose what she should wear, and he never objected to the fact that she never spoke or offered an opinion when other people were present, except to agree with whatever was said about the weather or clothes or children.

"No, no. I'm glad when you tell me what to do." Still,

she was unhappy. How was she to explain that when she couldn't understand it herself?

"Richard—" No, she couldn't.

"What do you want to tell me?"

"You'll be angry. I don't like to make you angry."

"For God's sake, I won't be angry. I promise."

"All right, Richard. I'll tell you. I want to believe in something."

"In what?"

"I don't know. Now you're angry with me."

He shook his head tiredly. "Honey, I'm as fucked up as you are right now. I'd like to believe in something, too. I used to have a mind. I haven't opened a book in ten years. I read the *Wall Street Journal* and *Barron's*. I can't even fuck right. I'm jerking off my life until I'm dry. Do you know what that priest asked me?"

Sally shook her head. She had never heard him speak like this before. It frightened her.

"He asked me whether I believed in God. Can you imagine? He asked me whether I believed in God."

She was afraid to mention that Sister Brody had asked her the same thing. She thought that perhaps that was a question priests had to ask, and she wondered what he had replied and why the question had upset him so. She felt drawn to him, and she went to him and put her cheek against his breast, and he put his arms around her and kissed her forehead and whispered, "Go up to bed, honey."

"I want you to come with me, Richard."

"I'll be up later."

"Then I'll read in bed until you come up."

"Sure."

"I might fall asleep. Please wake me up if you want me."

"Yeah, I'll do that."

She went to the stairs and started up. Then she turned and looked back at him, and he thought he saw tears in her eyes. Then she went on up the staircase.

Richard went into his study. He had formed the habit, when he was troubled, of sitting down at his desk and thumbing through his book of investments. This was a large, leather-bound loose-leaf book, which he kept locked in his desk, that listed every stock and bond and every other investment and real-estate interest that he had; his net worth, according to the vagaries of the market, varied from $100 million to $120 million. He had a mathematical mind and he could follow day-to-day changes almost to the dollar. There were more wealthy men than he in Greenwich, but he had come late to the game, leaving government because there was no money in it, no real money, bribes and tidbits here and there, but no real money.

But tonight, he didn't unlock the drawer. Tonight, everything was different, everything had changed; and behind this change was the dawning realization, a tiny possibility at first if indeed even that, growing and taking over his whole consciousness, first the notion, then the putting aside of the notion, then the growth of the notion, then his talk with Monsignor Donovan, and now its acceptance: Larry was coming here to kill him.

Or was he? What then? How could he be sure? He had never given much thought to death; for his age, he was a healthy man, no trouble with his heart or his blood pressure; he had a physical every three months and he came out of each with flying colors. He kept in shape, limited his drinking, and played golf and tennis. Sally had often remarked on what a fine body he had, and while much of his hair was turning white, he had lost very little of it.

Now he sat at his desk, and a cold chill took over his body. What was death? Dark and endless? He braced himself and whispered, "Fuck Larry. Fuck the whole lot of them. It's over, it's done with, it's long, long ago, and nobody gives a damn."

He always kept half a million in cash in the big safe behind the shelves of books that weren't books. If Larry had a gun—oh, bullshit! Larry was a onetime congressman, not a killer. He'd probably say, "We want you out of the country, Richard. Take that gorgeous wife of yours to the Cayman Islands and live a little."

Still, the cold chill of death would not leave him. His thoughts turned to Sally—what in hell would she do if he died? How could she deal with it? He had a trust fund of twenty million or so for Dickie—not that the little bastard deserved it—and the rest went to Sally. His lawyer, Jim Cartwright, had objected strenuously. "You have a place and a name in the community. You have to leave something to charity."

"I earned the money. It's mine. I can afford to pay you four hundred an hour, that's what money does for me. If Sally leaves me—well, we have the prenuptial agreement. If she stays, she gets it. I want it that way."

Money—for God's sake, did any of them understand money? . . . And how much would it take to buy Larry? The half million in cash that he kept in the big safe? The monsignor had asked him whether he believed in God. If God moved the world, God was money. He had never known anyone who didn't believe in money—except Sally. Why did he think that? He never overestimated Sally, yet he was never able to say to himself, simply, that she was stupid. She never asked for anything. He bought her gowns, jewels, fur coats, and she always thanked him.

Castle had no mother, no father, no sisters, no brothers. He stood alone in the world, and he had always stood alone. He made his own decisions. He condemned himself for having a moment of sheer stupidity, to confess to a priest. He owed Monsignor Donovan for not allowing him to speak. The ten thousand dollars was nothing.

He calmed down now. In a few minutes he would go up to bed, and Sally would be waiting for him. No one gave a damn for the dead; they might pile on the bullshit, but bullshit was bullshit. He might have put together the plan to get rid, once and for all, of those crazy Jesuits who were screwing up the works in El Salvador, and it was his written decision that the bishop had to go. He could make a decision; all his life he had made decisions, and there was hardly a ripple in the media when the bishop was shot. Even Drummond had wavered, but he had decided, and he had said, "Let's do it and get it over with and put the fear of God into them."

The truth is that then he didn't even know what a Jesuit was or what a bishop was, except that they were commies and working hand in hand with a commie movement. Now all that had changed; everything had changed. And Larry? Larry, he decided, needed money. Those fuckin' politicians always needed money. No matter how much you gave them, it was never enough, and if it weren't for that damn story in the *New York Times,* the notion that Larry was going to kill him would never have entered his mind.

He put it all away, all the ideas and fears of death, and started to go upstairs. There was nothing like a woman, naked in bed with you, to put away fear of death.

And then the doorbell rang.

It startled him and stopped him. Who on earth could be ringing his bell at this hour, already almost midnight? If it were one of those snotty kids that Dickie ran around with, he'd catch hell. He had warned Dickie about his friends showing up at all hours of the night, kids who had no sense of time. He switched on the outside lights and looked through the small iron grill, seeing two policemen and their car, lights flashing, in the driveway behind them. He opened the door to let them in.

"Late call, Mr. Castle," one of them said. "I hate to bust in on you like this, but we got orders to pick up your son."

"Dickie? For what?"

"Is he home, Mr. Castle?"

"He's home. I heard him come home about two hours ago. What in hell are you talking about?"

"The way I understand it, Mr. Castle, he was out with his girlfriend, and they had some kind of a fight and he messed her up. They had to take her to the hospital."

"For what? Is she claiming he raped her?"

Wrapped in a pink silk robe, Sally came down the big curved staircase that led to the floor above. "What happened, Richard?"

"You tell me, Oscar," Castle said to the officer. "You

know Dickie. He's a little wild, but he wouldn't rape any-one."

"It's not rape. They're not making any claim of rape. Like I said, he pushed her around and sprained her shoulder and put some scratches on her face, but her father's sore as hell and he wants to charge Dickie. The sergeant told us to bring him in."

"Whose kid is it? Who's her father?"

"Frank Manelli, the plumber."

"Oh, my God," Sally said. "I had Frank out here this afternoon. He doesn't want to arrest Dickie."

"I'm afraid he does, ma'am."

The other policeman said nothing. Sally was surprised at how calmly her husband was taking all this.

"What does it come down to?" Castle asked.

"We read him his rights, bring him in, and then there's a hearing tomorrow, and I suppose there'll be a fine, and maybe he gets some community service hours or maybe Manelli will calm down and forget the whole thing."

"I'll go upstairs and get him," Castle said.

"Let me go," Sally said.

"No, I'll go," and he started up the stairs.

Dickie was in bed, watching television, the sound turned low, and he switched it off with the remote as his father entered the room. Castle caught a glimpse of a porn film, but just a glimpse. Dickie was a good-looking boy, blond hair and blue eyes, and an innocent expression as he faced his father, brows raised inquiringly.

"What's up, Dad?"

Castle was strangely calm. "Get dressed," he said. "There are two cops waiting for you downstairs." Strangely calm, because under other circumstances he would have blasted the boy with anger.

"Cops?"

"Cops. They've come to arrest you."

"For what?" Dickie cried indignantly. "What did I do? I been right here in bed."

"For beating up Frank Manelli's kid."

"I didn't beat her up! I swear to God I didn't beat her up. I didn't touch her. All I did was grab her arm!"

"You're stupid, Dickie. What's her name and how old is she?"

"Her name's Christina."

"How old is she?"

"I don't know, fifteen, sixteen. But I didn't touch her."

"Yeah, like Clinton didn't touch Monica. You stupid little bastard. You're lucky it's a couple of cops and not Manelli downstairs. Did you fuck her?"

"No! I swear I didn't. She jumped out of the car into a stone wall and scratched her face. I didn't do that. All I did was grab her arm."

"Was the car moving?"

"No, we were parked."

Castle looked at Dickie thoughtfully and shook his head. Dickie and his friends always puzzled him, rich kids, the generation gap, the language they spoke. His son's mother was on drugs and going downhill quickly, and she had readily surrendered Dickie to his father. Castle paid her ten thousand a month in alimony, but it was Sally who had gently persuaded him to have the boy live with them. The very fact that he had grown up apart from Castle contributed to the lack of feeling on the part of both of them.

Now Castle said, "Finish dressing."

They went downstairs together.

"We're not going to arrest him," Oscar had decided. "We'll just take him downtown and maybe in the morning, it can be worked out."

"Do you mean that you'll put him in jail overnight?" Sally asked woefully.

"The cells are clean. You can come along with him, if you want to, Mr. Castle."

Dickie looked at his father pleadingly, but Castle shook his head. "You'll take good care of him. I'll be down tomorrow." And turning to Dickie, "Consider it a lesson in propriety."

"Oh no," Sally pleaded. "Does he have to go to jail?"

"The sergeant said bring him in. I don't know where else he can sleep downtown. We won't book him until Mr. Castle sees him tomorrow." Then Oscar said to the other officer, "Take him out to the car and make him comfortable."

Tears in her eyes, Sally watched Dickie walk out with the officer.

"Go back to bed," Castle said. "I'll come up in a few minutes."

She obeyed him without further question. She always obeyed him.

Castle took out his wallet and removed two hundred-dollar bills.

"This is not a bribe," he said, "and split it with the other officer. It's a small gratuity for the way you're running this. You could have come down hard and you didn't. He needs a lesson. Tell the sergeant I'll see him tomorrow."

Castle stood in the foyer for a few minutes after the police car had driven off, reflecting on the fact that during all the years of a very active life, he had never been arrested. He felt a touch of sorrow for his son, thinking that this was not the first time Dickie had been in trouble and it wouldn't be the last. Anyone who was so bereft of common sense that he would come on to a straitlaced Italian working-man's fifteen-year-old daughter would walk into anything. He didn't particularly like Dickie, who had come to him at age twelve, after five years of separation. They never talked, father and son, the way he had seen it done in movies, and that had never troubled him.

Finally, he went up to the bedroom.

Sally, still in her robe and sitting on a chaise, asked a question she had rehearsed several times in her mind: "Why did you let them take him away, Richard?"

"What else could I do?"

In her mind, Sally had formed another question: Why didn't you go with him? But she couldn't bring herself to say it. Instead, "What did he do, Richard? Was it bad?"

"He swore he didn't rape her or do anything else except tug on her arm to keep her in the car. They were parked alongside a stone wall. She jumped out of the car into the wall and scratched her face."

"Then why did they take him away?"

"I don't know all the details, Sally. Tomorrow, we'll go down to the police station and work it out."

Sally nodded, slipped out of her robe, and crawled into bed. She had already dried her eyes and removed the little makeup she used, and when Richard lay down beside her, she folded herself into his arms. He held her to him for a few minutes and then asked her whether she was cold.

"No. You know, the air-conditioning gets stronger at night. Shall I turn it down?"

"No, I'll let your body warm me."

Her body did warm him, but he felt that his soul was encased in ice. It was an odd feeling, for he had never thought of himself before in terms of having a soul.

Nineteen

Mary Greene and her husband, Herbert, had left the Castles' shortly after Harold Sellig had excused himself to join his wife at the hospital. Herbert admitted to Mary that the dinner party had not been half bad, certainly not as boring as he had expected it to be. Mary was driving. She slowed down and said, "That's being ungracious. You always make a thing out of seeing the Castles, as if you were doing them some great extraordinary favor."

"And you're slowing down to order me out and make me walk home. Is that it?"

"It's a thought. No, there's something wrong with the car."

"There's nothing wrong with the car. You're in low gear."

"Thank you. And one day, you'll be the designated driver."

"But you never drink. It's an act of pure charity."

"What? My not drinking?"

"No. Your driving." He added, "And my eyes are getting rotten. I dislike night driving."

"And my eyes?"

"You're nine years younger than I."

"Oh, I know. As a matter of fact, you do remind me of that now and then. I should warn women about marrying a man a decade older than they are: He can't drive at night because his eyes are getting bad. He can't lift things because his back is going. He can't remember things because his memory is going—"

"My memory is fine, and you know it. As for my back— have I ever whimpered about my back? All right, I enjoyed tonight. Sally Castle is one of the prettiest women I have ever seen—"

"Oh, thank you. When do men grow up?"

"They don't have to grow up if they marry the right woman."

"Deeper and deeper, Herb."

"All right, I don't like rich men. That's generic. I'm what they call an old lefty. I have a reputation for that, which I feel I must preserve. The voices of reason become quieter and quieter. And in apology for my remark about a woman being beautiful, I did like Sister Brody. She is something. If there were a million like her, the world would change its axis."

"And the monsignor?"

"Ah, there's a man I'd like to talk to and get his careful guard down. A very interesting man. Do you know him well enough to invite him to dinner?"

"I think so. But we can't afford Abel Hunt."

"A great man in his own right," the professor acknowledged. "The French understand that food is the essence of civilization, not computers but food, and when food is like what we ate tonight, we perform an exercise in civilization."

"Wow!" Mary exclaimed. "That's the most astonishing explanation for stuffing yourself that I ever heard."

"Thank you. But to get back to Donovan and Sister Brody, there's something happening in that church of yours that boggles my mind. I recall that years ago when Heywood Broun joined the Catholic Church, his Wasp friends came down on him like a ton of bricks, and his answer was that when the Church Militant begins to march, you'll feel the earth shake."

"Wow again. But who was Heywood Broun?"

Herb sighed. "Who was Heywood Broun? Not surprising in a country with a twenty-four-hour memory, but you're a teacher of children, a molder of young minds—"

"Herb! Get off it!"

"All right. He was a lefty newspaper columnist at the old *New York World,* if my memory serves me. My dad never missed his column."

"May he rest in peace. Meanwhile, you're right and wrong about what is happening to our church. We have a pope who is a great and brave man, and he has shaken the world a little, and we have a lot of people like those two you met tonight. We also have a lot of people who are not like them and would like to toss them out on their derrieres, given the chance. Someday, God willing, the Liberation Church and the Catholic Church may become the same thing—maybe someday."

They were at home now, and Mary steered the car into the garage. Theirs was an old Victorian house, which they had bought years before for thirty-nine thousand dollars and since then poured a goodly part of their savings into it. Now hardly a week passed without some Greenwich realtor begging to sell it for a million dollars plus. Such was the fate of real estate in Greenwich, Connecticut. At some point, starting about two decades ago, for reasons both arcane and evident, Greenwich had become the place where rich people preferred to live. Evident was the fact that it was only an hour from New York by car, less by train. Arcane, because no one ever can explain why a suburban town becomes *The Place.*

Both Herbert and Mary loved the house the first time

they saw it; Mary because it reminded her of her childhood home in Springfield, Massachusetts, and Herbert because of the porch, an old-fashioned porch that covered the whole front of the house and half of each side as well. The porch induced euphoric dreams of a time gone by, when people sat on their front porches and nodded and exchanged the time of day with their neighbors, while other people in buggies drove by. Of course, he was not old enough to have seen any of this, except in films and old engravings; nevertheless, it captured his heart and he refused to have the porch screened in and insisted on rocking chairs and wickerwork couches and grass rugs.

As they came onto the porch this evening, there was his cigar where he had left it, and as he picked it up, Mary said, "Oh, no, you're not going to smoke that wretched thing now before we go to bed."

"Not from your tone—absolutely not." He returned it to the ashtray. Inside the house, the telephone was ringing.

"I'll get it," Mary said. "Who could be calling at this hour?"

"Thank you, my dear, I love you," Herb replied, dropping down on the wicker sofa and stretching his legs. It was a beautiful, clear night, a full moon high in the sky, and the temperature about seventy degrees. He was a contented man, he told himself, and his lot was all that any man could desire. He had a wife he loved, a daughter who was either upstairs in bed or in the arms of some young lover and who was a pre-med sophomore at Yale, and a son who was a solid, decent young man—all of it so different from Castle, who had fathered a young scamp, already making a nasty reputation in town. He thought about Castle now and admitted to himself that in all truth he had misjudged him. Castle had been a charming host, offered the best of food and drink, as well as a Cohiba, something he had never smoked before. And his wife—well, she was obviously a trophy wife, but a real strawberry blond, and one had to give him credit for buying the best in the market. She was sweet and gentle and obedient; and while he loved

Mary, no one ever gave her points for obedience, although she had her moments of sweetness. She was a handsome, sharp-nosed Irish Catholic, and his mind went off, wondering why so many Jewish men, like himself, married second-generation Irishwomen; and then his thoughts turned to Harold Sellig, an interesting man, no one you would think of as a Vietnam veteran. He had read one of Harold's best-sellers that had been made into a successful film, enriching its author beyond measure, a book dismissed by Herbert as a contrived adventure-romance of no particular worth. His own books on linguistics had sold a few thousand copies and brought him a few thousand dollars, pedagogical tomes, yet he felt no envy and liked the fact that Harold Sellig looked so much like pictures he had seen of Gilbert K. Chesterton. Sellig's theory of universal guilt fascinated Herbert. Some months ago, Sellig had sent him a more recent draft of the manuscript; but as with so many manuscripts sent to him, he had put it aside and never read it. He decided that he would read it now.

At that point in his musing, Mary came out of the house, her face bleak. Thinking immediately of some family tragedy, Herbert leaped to his feet and went to her. "What happened?"

"Seth Ferguson is dead." Her eyes filled with tears. "He died tonight on the operating table."

Herbert embraced her. "That good, sweet man."

"Hold me tight, Herb, very tight. I love you. Don't ever die on me. I'll never forgive you if you do."

"I promise," he said.

"Sellig said Seth had talked of the operation as a lark. He'd be back in the office in a week. Have you Kleenex or something in your pocket?" He gave her a handkerchief, and she wiped her eyes.

"How old was he—seventy or so?"

"Too young to die," Mary said.

"Who called?" Herb asked her.

"David. He's staying over at Nellie's place, and they both want to come here for breakfast. It's Saturday and

Nellie's off. David says they have important matters to discuss with us."

"Oh?"

"I think they're going to tell us that they want to get married."

"Come on. You're jumping to conclusions. He's only twenty-one, and he has a year of college to finish. She's older, isn't she?"

"Twenty-three or twenty-four."

He shook his head. "We'll see. Seth Ferguson, what a loss, what a shame!"

"Come to bed, Herb, I want to crawl into your arms."

Twenty

By midnight, Frank Manelli's anger had cooled. His three kids were in bed, and he sat in the kitchen with his wife, Connie, drinking hot chocolate and munching one of her delicious raisin-and-oatmeal cookies. She had read somewhere that hot chocolate, made with milk, was a beneficial thing at bedtime. Frank was tired; usually he was in bed by ten and up at six, but this was Friday night, and he was determined to take no calls the following day, unless it was the most dire of emergencies. "And say a prayer that nothing happens tonight, no flooded bathrooms, no broken pipes. I've had it today."

"You got it," Connie agreed.

"They don't even call doctors anymore in the middle of the night."

Smiling, Connie nodded. "You know what Father Garibaldi said to me? He said that plumbers and electricians were the rock of civilization, and without them, our civilization might well collapse."

"Come on."

"And speaking of doctors, Dr. Ferguson died tonight."

"No! Where did you hear that?"

"Bella Santini called me. Her daughter's a nurse at the hospital."

"Why?" Frank growled. "Why? Why is it always the good guys?"

"God has his reasons."

"I'd like to have a few words with that God of yours."

"He's your God, too, Frank, and Sunday they're having a mass for him, and I want you to go. You missed the last two Sundays."

"I had emergencies."

"You have too many emergencies on Sundays, Frank. I hate to bug you, but you do."

"All right, all right, I'll go."

The kitchen phone rang, and Connie grabbed it, listened a moment, and said, "I'm so sorry, Mrs. Weatherall, but he's sleeping and he's exhausted, and I just can't wake him." A pause. "Yes, I can understand. You can try an all-night service. I'm sorry."

"What?" Frank asked.

"She can't turn off her sprinkler system, and she says everything will be flooded by morning."

"I hate this damn town!" Frank exploded. "It's a place of rich, stupid assholes."

"Frankie, don't talk like that, even when the kids are not around."

"Yeah. And when it rains all night, what's the difference? She lives way out, almost at Banksville, thirty minutes. I came into her place one morning, about eleven. Her sink had a drip. Her husband was in New York. There was a guy in her bed, and she comes out in a robe that left nothing to my imagination. The guy in bed is on his face, the sheet pulled up, and she tells me her husband didn't go to New York today. Then this guy speaks to her with a foreign accent. I know her husband don't have no foreign accent. He says the drip is driving him crazy. She don't give a damn what I see or know."

"And you had a good look at her, of course."

"Connie, what do I do? Close my eyes? I look, that's all. You know that."

"I know, I'm sorry, Frankie. I have no right to criticize you. I just lied like a trooper."

"Better than Clinton, I tell you that."

"I'll go to confession."

"Jesus God, Connie, you never done anything wrong in your life. Every week, it's confession."

"I do things wrong. If I were a good mom, I'd have known that Christie had a date with the Castle boy, and I would have kept her home."

"Come off that," Frank said. "You're a good mom, the best, and I love you."

"Yes, and what are you going to do about Dickie?"

"I don't know. Twenty years ago, I would have beaten the shit out of him, and I guess I'd still be in jail."

"Twenty years ago, you had just come back from Vietnam, and Christie wasn't even born yet."

"I thought of suing him and his father, but Abel says that any kind of a lawyer charges at least three hundred an hour—can you imagine? Two hundred seventy dollars more than I make an hour. The kid's spending the night in jail, and that'll teach him something, and I don't want no feud with Castle, and I like his wife. She's dumb but pretty—"

"I never knew a woman you didn't like."

"Is that bad? I'm Italian, you want me not to like women? I don't come on to them. You know that. And Dickie—what the hell, Christie's all right. I'll just drop the charges. I'll go to mass with you and the kids, day after tomorrow, but no confession. What am I going to tell the priest, that I'm Italian? He knows that."

Twenty-one

Dickie sat alone and forlorn in the holding cell at Greenwich police headquarters. It had been a quiet night, and in the course of things, there was little common crime in Greenwich, often no more than a dozen arrests in a week, most of them for drunken driving or petty theft. When it came to millions of dollars, the criminal record was longer and more interesting, but the movers in this increasing list of multimillion-dollar crimes and litigations never saw the inside of Greenwich police headquarters.

Dickie was frightened, because he had no idea of what awaited him. He had tried to glean some information from the two officers who had arrested him, but they were close-mouthed and gave little. The one instance he had experienced in his past was for disturbing the peace, when he and three of his friends had too much beer and had marched down Greenwich Avenue at two o'clock in the morning, when Greenwich Avenue is like a graveyard, shouting and singing at the top of their lungs. Then they were picked up, taken to the police station, where their parents were called to come and get them and pay their fines. This time was different. Dickie knew that he was being charged with assaulting an underage girl. He knew very little about the law, but the word *assault* terrified him. He never read newspapers, but watching network television, he had seen many an assault case punished with years of imprisonment. What would he do if they sent him to jail for five years? Five years was an eternity. He had heard, via TV and film, about young men made slaves of the tougher prisoners, raped and beaten, and sometimes killed. Whether this would happen to him in a Connecticut prison, he did not know, but his imagination ran wild. He was seventeen, too old to be tried as a juvenile? He didn't know.

Finally, past two in the morning, he fell asleep on the hard bench in the holding cell.

Twenty-two

Sister Patricia Brody, Harold Sellig, and Frank Manelli all had one thing in common: They all had bad dreams, which were sometimes unbearable nightmares. They all woke up in the morning, sweating and shivering.

The dreams of Manelli and Sellig were of Vietnam; the nightmares of Sister Brody were of El Salvador.

Some months ago Sister Brody had spoken about her dreams to Monsignor Donovan, who had a degree in psychology from Fordham University.

"They are nightmares of a sort, but without the distortions that usually come with nightmares. Oh, yes, some distortion, but very repetitive of what actually happened.

"It was in San Salvador, at a school. I was there with three lay workers and six Jesuit priests. You know what happened."

"Yes, but from your point of view?"

"I was in the school, and the priest and I heard the shots. The lay workers hid in a closet. I remained in the doorway. I was frozen there. I saw one of the Jesuits lying on the ground. He was dead. A priest ran toward him, and there was a burst of fire from another soldier who had an assault weapon. It literally tore him in half. The soldier was no more than twenty feet from the priest. In my memory, things come into focus, one by one. Another Jesuit was on his knees, his palms pressed in prayer, his head bent. Another soldier, standing behind him, was laughing."

"You remember that bit, laughing?" Donovan asked.

"I'll never forget it. It appeared that everything was happening at once, total insanity. A Jesuit who was with a class came to the door, right beside me, shouting in Spanish, 'Stop! Stop!' Then the soldier who was laughing emptied his pistol into the priest's head, the whole magazine, and blew the priest's head off. Then they shot the Jesuit standing in the doorway, beside me. They killed six of them—six Jesuit priests, the whole staff of the school."

"And still you didn't try to run away?"

"I was frozen with fear."

"And then?"

"And then they raped me. I don't know how many of them—I fainted after it began—and when I regained consciousness, there was blood all over me and dead priests everywhere. I don't know why they didn't kill me, but I suppose that for some reason they wanted a witness to what happened. I spent a week in the hospital, and that was when the dreams began."

It was three months ago that she told this story to the monsignor. By now, in June of 1998, the dreams came infrequently, yet each time she went to bed, it was with the prayer that the dream would not come. On this Friday night, after the dinner party at the Castles', Sister Brody felt a melancholic sense of peace. She felt that she had helped Sally, and that somehow Sally would begin to find a way. She rarely asked for anything when she prayed, and tonight, as she kneeled beside her bed, her thoughts were quiet.

Frank Manelli awakened at four in the morning, the usual time, whimpering, his knees drawn up in a fetal position, and Connie put her arms around his huge bulk and whispered to him, "It's all right, Frankie. I'll never let anything hurt you. It's all right, my baby. It's all right, and God watches over us."

"Sure, sure, honey." He relaxed, and in a few minutes he was asleep again. But Connie found it difficult to go back to sleep. She lay beside the warm body of her husband, wondering, as she had a hundred times before, why God and the Mother of God, whom she loved so much, had allowed this to happen, had sent a generation of young men into hell, with a punishment that would never end.

Harold Sellig did not sleep that night. He dozed now and then, but for most of the night he was involved with his thoughts. He loved Seth Ferguson, and he tried to think of his life with Ruth without the old doctor. No more long discussions about the wonders of the human body, no more reflections on the nature of the universe, no more of the comfort of having a father, of the feeling that both he and his wife were children of the same father. Harold had never in his life asked anyone for money. After the navy, he reached a point when they were broke; they never said a word to Seth or even allowed him to suspect, but it was Christmastime, and on that morning they found a small box under their tree with five hundred-dollar bills in it. They argued about it, but Ruth convinced Harold that if they returned it, Seth would be hurt beyond measure.

And now, Seth was dead.

Like most people without church or religion, Harold Sellig spent a great deal of time speculating about God.

Since Seth was no more a believer than he was, they felt a freedom to discuss God that most religious people lacked. God, like money, was something one never mentioned. One of Seth Ferguson's hobbies had been the early Greeks and the golden age of Athens. The Greeks of that time also argued about the gods, but they solved the perversities of chance and nature by creating a set of myths that gave the gods of Greece all the inconsistencies of human beings, all the jealousies and rivalries that they knew as a part of mankind's makeup.

Unfortunately, as Harold pointed out to Seth, monotheism put an end to that, although Seth countered with the fact that the small gold caduceus that his wife had given him when he graduated from medical school was the winged staff of the god Mercury—oddly enough the symbol of his profession.

They both stumbled over ethics, and tonight, half awake, Harold brooded over ethics. Why does a good man die so meaninglessly? Why are half a million people in Africa murdered by people so indistinguishable from themselves? The trouble was that, like so many disbelievers, he had come to the conclusion that there had to be a mind, a force, an intelligence—but what kind of an intelligence? Could Seth Ferguson's death be as meaningless as the death of an ant he stepped on? Harold had written a book about the ethics of mankind and had woven a net of guilt around the citizens—mostly very ordinary citizens—of the town he lived in, Greenwich, Connecticut. It was a pretty town, a decent town, well-kept, reasonably well-managed, perhaps with more than its share of wealthy people, but with middle-class people and very poor people as well. Seth had liked the manuscript and agreed with the concept—but who else? His wife, Ruth, rejected it, lumping it together with the widely held Afro-American accusation that every white was a racist.

Seth had said to him, "If this idea of yours, Harry, ever gained real acceptance, it would shake the world." But that was a sort of intellectual hubris. Nothing shook the world.

A week from now, no one but he or Ruth would even mention Dr. Ferguson.

People died, and if the dying was not close, nobody actually gave a damn. The newest theory was that there were too many people for a small planet. That was why so few of the rich in Greenwich cared about HIV. They gave much more money for other diseases in this Republican stronghold. HIV victims voted Democrat, anyway.

Then he threw that kind of thinking away. Ruth, lying beside him, had taken a sleeping pill, and now she was pressed up against him, her arm over his shoulder. The faintest light of dawn was in the sky.

He dozed off at last, and he dreamed. It was the day after the Tet offensive, and the black body bags were lined up as far as he could see, far into the distance, piled up over the broken buildings and the smashed tanks and guns.

PART TWO *Saturday*

Twenty-three

Larry, whose full given name was Latterbe in honor of a Civil War ancestor, Colonel Vernon Latterbe Johnson, was a meticulous man.

He was meticulous about everything. In his younger years and even in his childhood, he was neatly dressed, with a round face, blue eyes, and carefully combed corn-silk hair. People remarked that he had an innocent face. He grew into a tall, muscular six-footer, but he maintained the round face and the look of innocence. Thus, through his adolescence, he escaped blame for a number of things that he did. He also kept his weight down, and in college, he played football. He went to a small southern college. In a more prestigious school, he might well have graduated into a professional football player.

His father was a lawyer in the small southern town where Larry had been born. Larry spent two years working in his dad's office, and then, instead of going on to law school, Larry ran for sheriff. He was easily elected, and he served successive two-year terms. In the course of his first term, two men attempted to rob the local bank. Larry intercepted them as they came out of the bank, one of them holding an ancient hogleg six-shooter. Larry killed both of them with three shots. He had practiced with his .45-caliber automatic pistol for hours, and even though it was discovered the old six-shooter did not even have a firing pin, Larry was hailed as a hero and he received excellent coverage all over the state.

Larry felt a strange exultation in killing. It made him feel good, better than he had ever felt before: It made him feel like he had taken a snort of coke, something he had done occasionally, yet a practice he kept under strict control. He was much too meticulous to ever become an addict. During his second term, he was out in the woods hunting, when he came on a local black man fishing. Larry knew the man and did not like him, considering him one of those "uppity niggers."

"What are you up to, Cal?" Larry called out to the black man.

He turned his head to see Larry, and replied, "Fishing. Can't you see the rod in my hand?"

"Don't get snotty with me. Stand up and turn around."

Cal stood up and turned around.

"What's that you got in your belt?" Larry demanded.

"That's my fish knife."

"Show it to me."

"What for? Just an old fish knife."

Larry took out his .45. "I said, show it to me."

"OK, captain. You say, show it to me, I show it to you." Cal took the fish knife out of his scabbard, and Larry shot him, a single shot to the heart.

The black community raised hell over this killing, but the fish knife was grasped in Cal's hand, and Larry made sure that the hand was tightly clenched around it and ripped the front of his shirt to prove that Cal had come at him. The black community hired a lawyer from the capital city, but the case never went to trial, and Larry finished out his second term as sheriff.

It was this second killing that drew Hugh Drummond's attention. He came down to the little town that Larry ruled as his fiefdom, and they had a long talk in the sheriff's office. Drummond asked a series of questions about Larry's past, starting right at his birth and going into every detail. He then went into the record of Larry's father. When Drummond had telephoned to make the appointment, Larry asked some acquaintances in Washington about him, and he had good reason to respect Drummond and answer his queries.

Drummond liked him. His round, innocent face was good currency, and his southern accent was tempered by education. He smoked an occasional cigar and he confessed to his casual use of cocaine.

"No more," Larry said. "I gave that up when they elected me sheriff."

"Stick to that," Drummond said.

"Oh, yes, sir. I intend to."

"You drink?"

"Socially. A beer, not much more."

"You're not married. Are you gay? I want the truth."

Larry grinned. "You don't mince words, do you? I'm not gay. I'll give you some names if you want them."

"I'll take your word for it. How would you like to be a congressman?"

"I thought about it. I'd like it fine."

"I need a congressman. When I say I need a congressman, I mean exactly what I say. That little nigger you shot weighed one hundred and twenty pounds. You must be a hundred eighty."

"A hundred ninety-five."

"That incident defines where you stand on civil liberties, and today there's a lot of shit about civil liberties. You'll go

into the state legislature next year. I want you to file immediately. Consider it a postgraduate course. Get your name
around the district. Firm stand against busing and desegre-
gation, but do it with regret and class. You'll come up to
Washington, and I'll introduce you to a friend of mine,
Curtis by name. As for the word *nigger,* that's out of your
vocabulary. 'Negroes' from here on, or 'colored folk.' Curtis will introduce you to some of the right people and give
you a little training."

"Where's the money coming from? I can raise a few
thousand dollars, but not much more. These things take a
lot of money."

"Don't worry about the money. I'll take care of that. I
got a man in the state legislature, name of Ted James. He'll
be your top sergeant and he'll teach you the ropes. Believe
me, Larry, we don't sign contracts on this kind of thing.
Sam Goldwyn once said that a verbal contract is not worth
the paper it's written on. That was the movie business. This
is another kind of business entirely, so if we shake hands,
that's it. You want to think about it?"

"I thought about it," Larry answered, smiling. He had a
cherubic smile. He thrust out his hand, and Drummond
took it. Larry had a strong grip; Drummond's was stronger.

N ow, on this Saturday morning in June of 1998, Larry
was awakened by the hotel operator at 5:45. It was a lovely
morning, the sunrise streaked with thin lines of vapor
glowing in reds and yellows and violets. Larry stared out
of the window for a moment or two, thinking how odd it
was to see Lexington Avenue almost empty of traffic. Like
so many out-of-towners, he enjoyed the energy and excitement of New York.

He shaved carefully. He had a good head of hair, turning
white now, and his round face still bespoke innocence. He
put on a lightweight silk suit, a white shirt with thin blue
stripes, and a bow tie. He looked once more at the driver's
license and the American Express card that belonged to a

CIA man, whose name was Koles and who was fifty-five years old, wondering for a moment what name Koles was using on his mission to Latin America. His own wallet and identification, he sealed in a brown envelope. Then he examined the pistol and the silencer very carefully, even though he was quite familiar with the working of a .38 automatic. It had a full chamber. He dropped them into his jacket pocket.

Downstairs in the lobby, he smiled at the girl at the desk. "I'll be drifting around town today. I love to get up early and walk in New York, and the less I have on me, the better I feel. So put this in the safe, and I'll pick it up this afternoon."

"So do I," she agreed, "but I'm on the night shift, Mr. Johnson, and when I'm done, I don't feel much like walking. But the streets are much safer since Giuliani took over."

The breakfast room had just opened, and Larry always ate a good breakfast. After ham and eggs and fried potatoes, he felt ready for the day. He enjoyed the walk to the garage, and the car he had reserved was waiting for him. It was close to seven o'clock when he drove out of the garage.

Twenty-four

Monsignor Donovan was troubled when he awakened that Saturday morning, and since he was a man rarely troubled by either his beliefs or his actions, his state of mind was unusual. As was his daily habit, he awakened at six o'clock in his rather bare bedroom, adorned only with pictures of his mother and father and a carved crucifix given to him by a local bishop in South Africa. He shaved, showered, and dressed, and then he sat down on his bed and stared at the check Castle had given him—ten thousand dollars. The outreach of St. Matthew's always grew faster than its funds, and the church was always in debt. "You don't look a gift horse in the mouth" had been said to him so often that he hated the phrase; yet Sister Brody was right. He couldn't refuse the gift. But why had Castle given it? His wife? From what Sister Brody had told him, Richard Castle had little respect for the woman he had married, "a trophy wife," as the nun had put it, and Castle himself had not indicated any religious desire during their talk. At best, he felt that a Catholic priest was a willing receptacle for confession. He knew nothing about religion, less than nothing, thought the monsignor, recalling part of the talk around Castle's dinner table, when Castle asked him, "Just what exactly is a Jesuit? I know he's a priest." That followed the monsignor's mention that he himself was a Jesuit.

Having no desire to go into a lecture at the dinner table, Donovan simply replied that it was an order of priests devoted to education and to missionary work. Curiously, Castle had not followed up on the question when they spoke in the study. Something tugged at the priest's memory though, and he decided he would look into it before he deposited the check—at least sit down later, with youthful help, at the computer in the rectory and see what he might learn about Richard Castle.

Twenty-five

Richard Castle slept poorly. His was a carefully constructed world that he had planned for years. He was a good
salesman, who worked not with pressure but with enjoyable
persuasion. He had thrived as an investment banker and had
made money for himself and for his clients.

He was not the richest man in Greenwich, which was
probably a wealthier community than even Beverly Hills,
and he was still short of the billion dollars that had been his
aim when he hit sixty. Real-estate men had told him that he
could get four million for his home, but he had no desire to
sell. He belonged to the Hill Crest Club, and he had a beautiful wife. He had achieved all of the American Way of
Life, and he could buy anything he set his heart on. He
could even afford that ultimate of the wealthy man's desire, a private Learjet; but he disliked air travel and was
content with commercial first-class seating.

Yet he had a son who bitterly disappointed him and who was without either common sense or direction. For this, he blamed the boy's mother, his former wife, who had lost Dickie because of drugs and alcohol. Sally had passed the age of safe childbearing, nor was he sure that she could conceive.

As for Larry, well. he would take care of that in his own way. Larry loved money. Castle did not love money; he loved the power that money gave him. But Larry loved money the way a man loves a woman, or the way Drummond loved bulldogs. Castle was rarely introspective so he had created his self-image without ever realizing that he was creating it. He liked to think of himself as a country gentleman, and he had in his mind a picture of himself and Sally, two beautiful people riding horses together; but there was little room in Greenwich, particularly in his own patch of Greenwich, for horses, and he would live nowhere else. Once, the Back Country of Greenwich had consisted entirely of great estates, where there were broad pastures and plenty of room for horses as well as cattle, but that time was long gone. Anyway, he was not sure that he cared very much for horses as anything except a mental image; he preferred the fact of himself in a convertible BMW, of which he owned two, as well as a two-seater Mercedes and a Range Rover. He had decided that he would dock Dickie's car for a month; he could think of no worse punishment.

Finally, he fell asleep, with his alarm clock set for 6:50 A.M.

He woke of his own accord a few minutes before the alarm and immediately switched it off. In spite of the blinds and curtains, the bedroom was filled with a dusty light, and he turned to look at Sally, sleeping so peacefully beside him. Of all his possessions—and he saw her as such—he was most pleased with Sally. After all, she would be forty years old in the fall, and he had never seen a woman of her age who could match her looks. He knew he could have had his pick of any number of beautiful women between twenty and thirty, but he had no desire for a clone of the blond, blue-eyed, long-legged second wives that so many of his friends sported, and looking at Sally with her strawberry blond hair and translucent skin, he had a feeling of well-deserved superiority, not as a partner but as an owner. That she was meek and subject to any and all of his desires made no difference to him. She was his; and these reflections reminded him that he had made a sort of date with Muffy the night before.

Well, the hell with that, thinking of the times he had been to bed with Muffy, the hard-limbed emaciated body and the "augmented" breasts; she'd have a long wait before he'd call her again.

He left his bed quietly, went into their bathroom with its huge square tub, remembering a nasty crack he had once overheard in the locker room at Hill Crest, "Castle, his bathrooms have bathrooms," and then grinning with pleasure as the warm shower flowed over him. Then he shaved, went into the dressing room and pulled on a pair of blue jeans and a polo shirt, and put his bare feet into moccasins. That was his weekend dress, unless he had a luncheon or dinner date.

Rising early pleased him. Dickie never got out of bed before ten, and Josie would be up in a few minutes, at seven, to set for breakfast on the terrace during the summer weeks; and since it was Saturday, Sally had not set her alarm and would probably sleep until nine. She professed great sympathy for Dickie, but Castle wondered how real it was. Certainly, Dickie was far from pleasant to her.

Going to his study, Castle closed the door behind him. Then he pressed the button, hidden behind an etching, that moved the bookcase, revealing the safe. He twirled the combination quickly and pulled the heavy steel door open. Inside, there was a compartment, closed off from the rest of the safe, filled with packets of bills, in denominations from twenty dollars to five hundred dollars. The five-hundred-dollar bills were in packages of fifty, bound with a strip of tape, each representing twenty-five thousand dollars. Castle removed ten packages, two hundred and fifty thousand dollars, closed the compartment, closed the safe, and pressed the button that moved the bookcase back into place. Then he packed the bills into an old sport bag and left the house, still without seeing anyone or being seen by anyone.

In the part of the pool house that had been converted into his at-home office, Castle looked at his watch. It was a half hour past seven o'clock. He had a few minutes before he would walk down to the gate posts of his driveway and wait for Larry.

Castle had already made plans to take off with Sally if the need arose, but there was no indication, so far as he knew, that the newspaper investigation of what had happened in El Salvador had reached the point of a congressional inquiry. The Republicans, who controlled both houses of Congress, were too focused on Clinton and his sexual antics; and since some of what had happened occurred during a Republican administration, a public hearing of the case was the last thing they would look forward to. He had a small but elegant home in the Bahamas, where he was on good terms with most of the government. But that was a last resort.

He could think of only two reasons that Larry made the appointment. The most likely was that Larry needed money. The far reach was that Larry intended to kill him. Either way, he was confident that he could handle it. In any case, as his ace in the hole, he scribbled a note:

If I am found dead, my killer is a former United States congressman, name of Latterbe Johnson. He murdered me between eight and nine on the morning of June 20, 1998.

He quickly copied it, locked one copy in the drawer of his desk, a solid, stainless steel and rosewood desk and a drawer not easily opened, folded the original, and left it on his desk. He meant the note to be seen by Larry and no one else. Then he put on a light sweater that he kept in his office and walked down the long driveway.

Twenty-six

At seven-thirty on this Saturday morning, Nellie Kadinsky's alarm shrilled, and the two naked bodies on the bed stirred awake. It was warm in the room, and they had slept with only a sheet to cover them. Nellie had a tiny apartment in a frame house converted for nurses' occupancy about half a mile from the hospital. There was an old window air conditioner in the room; just enough air crawled in to make it sleepable.

"Up and out and get to it!" David usually awakened in high spirits. "They breakfast at eight-thirty."

Nellie moaned, "I have two lousy days off, and usually something happens on Sunday, and you're dragging me out of bed at seven-thirty."

"Doesn't anything happen in the line of disaster on Saturday?"

"Yes, it does."

"Then let's get out of here before you're called. Anyway, they're both teachers, very set in their habits. They'll get grumpy if they have to wait for us, and when we tell them, we don't want them grumpy."

"Wasn't your father a close friend of Dr. Ferguson?"

"He was our family doctor, yes. But I don't think they were close friends."

Nellie was sitting on the bed now, staring at David. He had a strong, tight body, a good athlete with a ruddy, freckled skin and reddish hair. "I asked you to marry me last night. How do you feel about that?" she asked.

"The same way I felt last night. The same way I felt since I met you. I begged you to marry me for two years. You didn't ask me. You finally said yes."

"And in three months, you go back to school in Cambridge, and I stay here."

"Four hours away."

"David, chronologically, I'm three years older than you. Actually, it's at least ten years."

David thought about that for a while, and then he nodded. "OK, if you're backing out, I'll wait."

"I don't want to wait, David. Let's go beard the lion and the lioness in their den."

He laughed. "Lion and lioness—no, it doesn't fit."

At eight-thirty, they were at the Greenes'. When they entered the house, David's sister, Claire, embraced Nellie and kissed her. "Morning beautiful lady. As for you," she said to David, "I never see you."

"I work."

"Ha!"

"That's expressive."

Claire, two years younger than David, dark-haired as her mother was and losing childhood fat to the strong bones of her face, led them into the kitchen. The Greene house had been built eighty years ago, at the tail end of Victorian construction, when kitchens were large enough for a big coal stove and a hot-water boiler as well. It had been modernized, but none of its size had been lost. It no longer contained the coal stove and boiler, but it had a worktable and enough room for a round table of heavy birch, where eight people could sit comfortably. It replaced the dining room, which had been turned into a library and study for Herb Greene and his wife.

Herb was at the table, reading the local daily newspaper, the *Greenwich Time,* which Mary slipped out of his hands as David and the two young women entered.

"Sorry," Herb said. "They're late."

"They're not late," Mary said.

Breakfast was an important meal at the Greenes'. They had eggs and bacon and waffles and hot rolls, yogurt and dry cereal and milk and coffee, everything put out and eaten in no particular order. Mary was not much of a cook, and being sensible, she stuck to what she knew and took the easy way out. They talked about Seth Ferguson, who had brought both David and Claire into this world, and there was some wiping of eyes.

"It's odd," Herb said, "that I should have met Harold Sellig last night for the first time. He was at the dinner party the Castles gave, and it set me to thinking about how things connect. His wife wasn't with him; she was at the hospital. I suppose you were there, Nellie?"

"Yes. I work with Dr. Loring."

"What exactly happened, if I may ask? I thought the heart bypass was a reasonably safe operation by now."

"I suppose it is," Nellie said uncertainly. "I don't like to talk about operations, if you will forgive me. I'm just a nurse, and I've only been an operating room nurse for a year, and I do take some courses and hope to be a physician one day. Dr. Ferguson's heart gave out. That was no fault of the surgeon. I'm just not equipped to say any more than that."

David watched her. He was going to speak, and then he decided not to say anything.

"I'm so sorry for Harold and his wife," Mary said. "They were very close to Dr. Ferguson."

"They both were devastated," Nellie agreed.

"Things connect," Herb Greene continued, taking up what he had said before. "Sellig sent me a copy of the manuscript of his new book about a month ago. I put it aside, meaning to read it and never finding time. When we got home last night, I picked it up again."

"When did you turn your light off?" Mary asked.

"About two. It's a short book. He calls it his Greenwich novel, 'The Assassin.' A very strange book about Greenwich. He holds that when someone is killed, we all bear responsibility, that in a sense every human being is an assassin. I squirmed a bit, but his net is too large."

"I should hope so," David said.

"I'd like to read it," Nellie said.

"I can live without that," from Claire. "I haven't killed anyone yet, but I have a physiology professor—well—"

"I've read it," Mary told Nellie. "You can have my copy."

Nellie wondered when her prospective mother-in-law had read it—perhaps with manuscript in hand while she was preparing breakfast. Then she rejected the thought. It was probably lying on the bed when she awakened. Nellie was intimidated by Mary, though Mary Greene, suspecting what was coming, was trying to be absolutely neutral—yet unable not to think of the old saw "A son is a son till he gets him a wife, a daughter's a daughter all of her life." Rising to refill the coffee cups, Mary picked up the manuscript, which lay on the kitchen counter.

"Here it is, and of course you can read it, Nellie."

Before Nellie could reply, David said, "Hold on," the last thing he wanted being a cross fire of politeness between his mother and Nellie. "We're here with breaking news. Nellie and I have decided to get married."

Silence around the board. Then Claire clapped her hands, lifted her orange-juice glass, still with half an inch in it, and cried, "Cheers."

No response. Nellie was thinking, Why, why did I let it happen this way?

"When did you decide this?" Herb asked.

"Last night. I know you're all surprised, but we've known each other for over two years and have been practically living together much of that time." David was serious, firm and unyielding. "We know each other, and we love each other."

Unexpectedly, Mary smiled. Nellie was sitting next to her. Mary leaned over and kissed Nellie. "Welcome, my dear," she said.

Herb said, "At this moment, I need my morning cigar. David, come out on the porch with me, and I'll treat you to one of my best Davidoffs."

"Now that's something to write home about," David said cheerfully.

Times do change, Mary thought. He tells his mother that he's been sleeping with a woman for two years. Well, what did I think when he didn't come home at night?

David followed his father into the study for the cigars and then out onto the porch, the only place where smoking was allowed. "This I enjoy," his father said. "There are only two times of the day when I really enjoy a cigar, after breakfast and after dinner. Your mother still shrinks at the thought. Now this one"—picking up the cigar he had left on the porch the night before—"I started because it never occurred to me that Castle would offer his guests real, valid Cohibas."

"No kidding? Why didn't you sneak me one? I never smoked a Cohiba."

"Bad manners, my boy. You don't steal cigars. And by the way, how much do you make down at the boatyard?"

"Six dollars an hour, nine when I work overtime."

"Your last year in college—you're majoring in biology. You still intend to follow research biology?"

"Of course. I know where you're going, Dad. Merck and Pfizer have already offered me jobs around the fifty-thousand-dollar level. I intend to take my masters at Yale and I'll get my doctorate during the years to come—both at night. It's rough, but Nellie is also taking night courses in medicine. So we'll manage. I've met a lot of women—I know what I want."

"I'm not arguing, just touching base. Does her family know about this?"

"Not yet, but she's her own woman."

"She's two years older than you."

"You're nine years older than Mom."

"She's Catholic, isn't she?" Herb asked.

"Non-churchgoing and I'm a non-synagogue-going Jew. As you know, that's a good combination."

Herb looked at his son thoughtfully, wondering why they had never had a talk like this before. He considered himself a reasonably good and intelligent father, reflecting that it was an odd kettle of fish that he had bred Claire, a firm Catholic, mass every Sunday with her mother—he went with them on Christmas and Easter—and David a firm nonpracticing Jew.

"When did you decide that you were Jewish?" he asked David.

"I stopped going to mass when I was eleven, I think. Mom never mentioned it or pushed me."

"She's a remarkable woman, Dave. Never sell her short."

"What do you suppose they're talking about in there?"

"Marriage. She's being charming to Nellie, starting out on the right foot."

"How do you know?" David asked.

"I know her. That's what makes a good marriage."

"Oh? Well, what do you think?"

Herb shrugged. "You could do worse."

"That's comforting. Nellie's a wonderful woman."

"Most women are. They have to be just to survive."

"I'll keep that in mind," David said. "Do you want to go inside?"

"Not until I've finished this cigar."

Twenty-seven

At eight o'clock that Saturday morning, with the whole Hunt family still asleep, the telephone rang. Abel stumbled out of bed to answer it, said, "Yes, hold on, I'll wake him."

The voice at the other end begged him not to wake his son and apologized for calling so early.

"Doesn't matter. He should be up, anyway." Abel put down the phone, walked to his son's room, shook him awake and commanded, "Get your ass up. Telephone for you."

"Who?"

"That priest from the church—Father Donovan."

Joe stumbled barefoot into the kitchen and picked up the telephone. Abel followed him, listening.

"Sure," Joe said. "I'll be happy to . . . no, no trouble at all. Be a pleasure." He put down the telephone.

"Now, you tell me," Abel said sternly, "what in hell a priest is doing calling you up at this hour in the morning?"

"He's not just a priest, he's a monsignor. Monsignor Donovan."

"And just what does this Monsignor Donovan have to do with you? Is he trying to convert you?

"No, no, absolutely not."

"Did you tell him you're a Baptist, born and bred out of generations of God-fearing Baptists, wholly immersed in your baptism and not just sprinkled with some holy water? Did you tell him that? Because if you didn't, I'll tell him myself."

Abel's wife, Delia, came into the kitchen at that point, and said, "What's all this shouting?"

"I'm not shouting." Joe grinned. "Dad's shouting."

"He's been baptized," Delia assured her husband. "You know that. You were there. That crazy preacher, your friend Ishmael, nearly drowned the boy."

"Look, both of you, Father Donovan does not want to baptize me. I give him computer lessons."

"You give him what?"

"Computer lessons. I teach him how to operate the church's computer."

"They got one of those devilish machines in the church?"

"They have one in the Castles' kitchen. Why not in a church? And it's not in the church, it's in the rectory."

"Why you?" Abel asked aggrievedly.

"Because I'm a hacker, a nerd, a computer wizard."

"How does he know that?" Abel asked suspiciously.

"Word gets around."

"Does he pay you?" Abel was still suspicious.

"Three dollars an hour. I won't take any more."

"You mean with all the money that church has, they don't pay you minimum wage?"

"They don't have any money. Anyway, I'm trying to teach you how to use our computer. I don't charge you."

"Room and board and college?"

"Exactly. So I don't charge you."

"Oh, leave the boy alone," Delia said. "They're good people, and it's nice that he helps them."

Twenty-eight

Ruth Sellig was up and making coffee when Harold awoke. Their house in Riverside—another part of Greenwich—was on a bluff overlooking Long Island Sound. It was an old, sprawling house with brown weathered shingles, and the tall glass doors that lined three sides of it were more California than New England coast. The kitchen looked out on the water, small, dancing waves in the morning sunlight. Here and there were the white triangles of small boats, either tied up to their buoys or running with the morning breeze. Harold's own little catboat was tied at the bottom of the bluff, and he looked at it regretfully thinking that Ruth would be in no mood for sailing this summer.

"I couldn't sleep," Ruth said. Her dark eyes were bloodshot, her face drawn and tired. "I got Oscar on the phone." Oscar was their son, just turned eighteen. "I tried him first in Paris, but the clerk at the hotel where he was staying said he had gone on to Lyons."

"Did you tell him?"

"I was going to, and then when I reached him, I couldn't. You know, Dad talked me into letting him go abroad for the summer. Do you know why he went to Lyons?" Her eyes filled with tears again.

"No. He wasn't supposed to."

"Well, you know how Dad never bought a dish or a pot after Mom died, and you know you break dishes and cups. Oscar decided to go to Lyons, where they're famous for their porcelain, and have a set made for Dad with a caduceus and Dad's initials—oh, damn it." Her throat choked up.

Harold put his arms around her. "Let's take the coffee and sit outside and have a smoke." He picked up the coffeepot and a couple of mugs. "Then, you didn't tell the kid?"

"I didn't have the heart to," Ruth confessed. "I know I should have, but, you know, he and Dad discussed this trip for weeks. They went over the maps, and Dad, I think, selected places he had always dreamed of but had never seen. Cornwall, for example. He always wanted to go to Cornwall but never gave himself the time. He never took a vacation. You remember?"

"Oh, but I do," Harold said. "I used to beg him. I said we'd both go with him. Last year, Oscar's last year of high school, I told him this was the perfect time."

"I remember. I remember what he said: Suppose someone gets really sick while I'm gone? His great grandfather came here from Cornwall. He was a doctor, Dr. Rowdy Ferguson. Can you imagine anyone giving a child that name?"

"No worse than Harold."

"I like your name."

"There goes Craydon's yacht," he said, pointing to an eighty-foot beauty putting out to sea.

Ruth began to cry. "Not over that stupid yacht, but here

we are, sitting and talking as if nothing has happened."

He rose and stood behind her, bending over and kissing the nape of her neck and folding his arms around her. "Seth knows how much we love him."

"To know, you have to be somewhere. Do you believe that nonsense?"

"Sometimes. When I want to believe it. Right now I want to believe it."

"We have to go down and see the undertaker," Ruth said, almost crossly.

"Time for that, Ruthie. He said he wanted to be cremated. Do we go along with that?"

"His living will included instructions for the hospital to take any organ they had any use for. He said there wouldn't be enough left for a proper burial. God help me, that's my father I'm talking about."

"It's better to talk about him, honey, than not to. We'll be talking about him for the next fifty years."

"Yes." She stood up and embraced him. "I need you, Harold. I'm not worth shit today. It took my last bit of strength to deceive Oscar."

"Why don't you lie down and get some sleep. I'll take care of everything."

"I won't sleep."

"Try. Lie down and close your eyes."

"All right, I'll try."

Harold went inside, found the sleeping pills, and put the container in his pocket, and then felt like a fool for doing so; yet he had never seen his wife like this before. She was always alive with energy. He had a theory about professional photographers, that they bristled with energy and moved like dancers. At least Ruth did. He was always amazed at her photographs—especially the way she put life into that little rabbit of a woman that Castle had married.

He watched her as she came inside. He was a chubby man, colorless hair and glasses, and three inches shorter than Ruth. He loved her, everything about her—her cynicism, her tall, hard body, just under six feet, her willingness to go anywhere and do anything to get the right picture. "If only I were with you in Vietnam," she had once said, to which he had answered, "Thank God you weren't."

Yet she had not said a word about the changes in his manuscript. What an utterly selfish hog he was, thinking about his damn book with poor Seth either lying on the autopsy slab or already shipped down to the undertaker without his liver or kidneys or anything else they found useful. And this was worse, standing and berating himself with his sharp whip of guilt.

Suddenly, Ruth appeared, now in a robe, and said, "Harry, with all this going on, I never told you. I read the manuscript over during those miserable hours of waiting. It's good—damn good."

And with that, she disappeared into the house and the bedroom.

Twenty-nine

At seven-thirty that morning, Sister Patricia Brody knelt by her narrow bed and prayed. Hers was a tiny room, eight feet wide, ten feet long. It contained only one ornament, a crucifix carved by a woodcutter in El Salvador. The single window in the room opened itself to the early sunlight, and in the broad beam of radiance, dust motes danced and plunged.

Her prayer was silent and wordless. She listened to the silence and allowed the silence to bring her where it might. The silence was an ocean of what was boundless, filled with mystery beyond the scope and reach of the human mind. Sometimes, once in a great while, she broke through that great barrier of silence and touched the wonder of what was and is and always will be, and then for at least a moment, she was filled with a joy that made up for all the misery and contradiction that encased her life. She had no description or understanding of this joy; there were no words for it in language available to her. She was a well-educated woman, college and postgraduate degrees in theology and psychology, and she had read a great deal about satori and enlightenment, but this moment of illumination was for her neither satori nor enlightenment. She had never spoken of it to anyone because she did not know how to speak of it.

Thoughts crossed her mind while she prayed and listened, and for the most part she threw them away; but this morning, Sally Castle intruded. Sister Brody had once been a slender and good-looking young woman, but with her middle years, any care about her appearance had slipped away. When she thought about beauty, it was not of the face or the body, but now the thought came to her that beauty, like that of Sally Castle, was not simply features or hair or body. Why had she been so drawn to Sally? What miracle could allow a woman to come out of the dregs and filth of a life as wretched as life gets in a place like California and at the age of forty be this gentle and soft-spoken person?

These questions interfered with her prayer, and she let them go and returned to the deep silence.

Thirty

Larry did not require directions, driving from New York City to Greenwich, Connecticut. He had been to Richard Bush Castle's home a number of times because Castle was always good for at least a hundred thousand in campaign money. He admired the great sprawling house that Castle lived in, his beautiful wife, his expensive cars, and his staff of servants, and he had always left there filled with envy. He himself kept a small apartment in Georgetown and a permanent address in his hometown, where he had inherited his father's house. It was one of the better houses in that town, but nothing at all compared to Castle's place.

He had sort of made up his mind that when he had three million socked away in his safe-deposit box and in quiet but good investments, he would phase out Drummond and live the kind of a life Castle lived. But for now he had to finish his ordeal over the documents Castle had foolishly put his name to. He was not a professional killer, but he had killed three men in his lifetime, and the memory of the rush and headiness that had followed those killings was like nothing else he had ever experienced. He looked forward to meeting Castle this morning with excitement and some fear—and also with some pride. There was pride in his admission to himself that he was a crazy bastard of sorts. It made him smile.

It was a fine morning, as fine as only a pleasant June morning can be. The trees were in full bloom, and the morning temperature was about seventy degrees. There was little traffic this early, and Larry never allowed his speedometer to pass fifty-five miles per hour. He had no desire to be stopped by a cop, with his CIA identification and a gun in his jacket pocket. He knew that Castle would note the bulge in his pocket, but Castle was slender and weighed no more than one hundred and fifty pounds. Larry could break him in two with his bare hands, if the occasion required.

And Larry had to admire Drummond and Curtis. They left nothing to chance, no stone unturned. Yet he had to keep in mind that they were dangerous. People who planned everything down to the last detail were always dangerous.

From the rental garage, Larry drove up to 97th Street, where he took the tranverse through Central Park to the Henry Hudson Parkway. He liked the drive along the Hudson River, and then the Cross County to the Hutchinson River Parkway and then the Merritt Parkway. His exit was North Street in Connecticut, and a mile more to Castle's driveway. As he turned into the driveway, between the two stone posts crowned with ornamental lights, he saw Castle walking down the driveway toward him. Larry pulled his car off the driveway onto the grass and got out of the car.

The two men shook hands.

"I'll forgive the wheel marks on my lawn, Larry," Castle said, "it's that good to see you." He noticed the bulging jacket pocket and said to himself, *Play this cool and easy. Don't get nervous. Money talks.*

"Sorry," Larry apologized. "I live in Georgetown, no lawns or wheel marks. Shall I pull off?"

"No. Let it be. The hell with the wheel marks."

"You're looking good," Larry observed.

Measuring the tenor of every word, Castle relaxed slightly. "Living the good life. It pays off," he said, smiling. "Suppose we walk up to my office—you know, the place in the pool house. We have to talk, and no one will interrupt us there. I also have a small gift for you."

"I never refuse small gifts or large ones. It comes with the territory."

As they walked toward the pool house, Larry said, "You read the story in the *Times*?"

"I did."

"Found it disturbing?"

"More or less," Castle replied, thinking that this was the game he had played for years. A company required so many millions of dollars, and you took it to a bank or a brokerage house and you convinced them that the stock was worth that many millions of dollars. What was his life worth, and why didn't he call the cops and get some protection or have them pick up Larry? But cops don't pick up a suspect on somebody's word, and he didn't want protection. And he wanted desperately to meet Larry and hear what he had to say, and maybe that bulge in his jacket was a cellular phone and not a gun; and Castle had thought of various responses to whatever situation was brewing in Washington, and he felt that Larry might have the answers.

He took the risk. Last night, for reasons he did not understand, he had almost blown it with his desire to talk to the monsignor—thinking that might open some door to him, but he preferred this risk. After all, what sense did it make for Larry to kill him? Larry had made no overt gesture, and all his life Castle had taken risks. He had floated Internet companies and other high-tech offerings that had never turned a profit and had no projected profits for years to come, and yet, by now their stocks had tripled for no good reason at all.

As they walked toward the pool house, Larry's thoughts took a different road entirely. It was many years since he had been sheriff and shot that black man, but he still remembered that cocaine-like high it had given him, that sense of ultimate power, the look on the black fisherman's face as his life departed, that stunned, unbelieving look.

He recalled a story he had read when he was very young. It concerned a king who had decided to kill a duke. He invited the duke to dinner, and course after course of delicious food was served, but no bread—and thus the duke realized that he would never leave the table alive, for the king would not break bread with someone he had decided to kill. Yet even though it was early morning, Castle might well offer Larry one of the Cuban cigars, with which Drummond kept his good friends supplied. Would he, Larry, accept a cigar?

But in the pool-house office, Castle produced a bottle of scotch whiskey and two glasses.

"Too early to drink," Larry said. He was looking at the desk, where the letter Castle had written was lying. He picked it up and read it. "What made you think I was coming here to kill you?" Larry asked.

"It's a possibility."

"And if so, what are you going to do?"

"Persuade you that your best interests lie elsewhere."

"Oh? And how?"

"Pick up that bag and open it," Castle said, pointing to the athletic bag. "No, Larry, I don't have a gun. No guns here or in my house. I hate guns."

Larry nodded, studied Castle thoughtfully for a long moment, and then lifted the bag to the desk. He unzipped it, picked up one of the bundles of money, riffled it, and pursed his lips.

"How much, Bush?"

"Two hundred and fifty thousand." Larry had used that intimate name. It might mean something or it might not. "All fifties, and it's clean money, Larry. I get the money nine thousand at a time, right under the limit. Been doing that for years. No numbers on the record, no fussing with the tax people. You don't have to report it. It's tax free. I know that two hundred and fifty grand is not Fort Knox, but there's more where it came from."

"It's mighty tempting," Larry agreed.

"You want me out of the way before a subpoena is served? There's a very simple way. I pick up Sally and some luggage and take off for the Bahamas. I have a house and a boat down there, and I can stay there for a year if I want to. I have a computer and I can do business there as well as here. They can't touch me or subpoena me there. I know all the top people in the Bahamian government and just how much money it takes to keep some of them happy. You want to visit me there—well, it's one hell of a sweet place. And I have dual citizenship, there and here."

"It sounds pretty good," Larry admitted. "Except for one thing."

"What's that?"

"What do I tell Drummond?"

"Fuck Drummond!"

"I'd like to, but—"

"But what?"

Larry shrugged. "He'll kill me if I don't kill you."

"Larry, you don't hate me."

"No more than anyone else."

"You can't kill someone in cold blood."

"Why not, Bush? Most killings are done in cold blood."

"Not by ex-congressmen. And why me? Why not Curtis? Why not you? What in hell makes Drummond decide to be an executioner? It's been years and years, and not even a whimper about it. Who the hell cares about it today? People don't even remember where El Salvador is. Who gives a damn?"

"Drummond. He wants to be governor."

"You're kidding. Governor of his state—with his past?"

"He's drying it up. By now most of it is dried up, and he has to dry up the rest of it."

"But why me?" Castle persisted.

"Bush, Bush, think about it. You were the one who was always yelling about the goddamn Jesuits. I don't think you knew what a Jesuit was. To you, like to everyone else in State, they were communists. They weren't communists, Bush, but you were too goddamn stupid to know that. You wrote the orders for the shooting—six of them. Roberto Aubisson is dead, but General García is alive and in protective custody. He was your contact, and he'll testify that the orders came from you. He'll talk about that Catholic bishop, Romero, you had shot, and the word is that he's going to put the murder of the nuns and the lay workers on your yellow ticket."

"I had nothing to do with the nuns!" Castle burst out. "You know that! That was Drummond's idea."

"Like you said, fuck Drummond. It's all your baby." Never taking his eyes off Castle, Larry took out his gun and the silencer, fixing the silencer in place.

"Larry, don't do this," Castle pleaded. "Don't do it."

Larry stuffed the letter Castle had written into his pocket.

"Larry, I sent a copy to my lawyer."

"When? You didn't know I was coming until last night. I looked in your mailbox at the road. No letter there. I got to do what I got to do. I'm sorry, Bush."

At that moment, the door to the office opened, and Josie, the downstairs maid, appeared in the doorway. Larry swung around, saw her, registered a black face and fired twice. Both bullets struck her chest, and Josie collapsed in the doorway. The thermos of hot coffee she was carrying dropped from her hand.

Castle leaped to his feet, yelling, "You dumb bastard, you didn't have to do that! You didn't have to kill her, you fuckin' prick! I faxed the letter in, you dumb bastard, I faxed it!"

Possibly Castle's last thought was, *Why didn't I fax it?* Then Larry fired, and the single shot hit his forehead just above his nose. His head snapped back, his legs crumpled, and he fell face forward, flat on the floor, a trickle of blood running from under his head.

And Larry asked himself, What in hell do I do now?

Moving like a man in a dream, he dragged Josie's body into the room, found a match in his pocket, and lit the letter Castle had written. He allowed it to burn on the metal top of the desk. He separated gun and silencer and put both in his jacket pocket. He closed the door and peered out of the window facing the house, seeing no sign of movement. It was a half hour after eight.

He looked around the room, trying to remember what he had touched. Where had he left fingerprints? On the desk? He wiped the desktop with his handkerchief, scattering the ashes of the letter on the floor. He tried the desk drawer, but it was locked. Decades ago, when he had been a sheriff, he had learned something about crime, but not much. He wiped the doorknob clean. Why hadn't he worn gloves? What else had he touched? The chair? He wiped the chair arms. He was drenched in sweat now, in spite of the air-conditioning that kept the room at a temperature of seventy degrees. Where was the rush, the cocaine-like high he remembered?

Then he went through Castle's pockets, and sure enough, there was the key. His hand was shaking as he opened the drawer. It contained a leather-bound date book, some papers clipped together. He went through them quickly, then dropped them to pick up a sheet of paper folded in half. This was pay dirt, the copy of the letter Castle had given him.

"Hallelujah!" Larry exclaimed. "Blessings to God or the Devil—I don't give a fuck which!" Then he burned it where he had burned the other copy.

He opened the door and looked around. Still, no sign of anyone. Then he remembered the athletic bag with the money in it. How could he have forgotten it? He picked up the bag and zipped it closed.

All he desired at the moment was to get out of there. He closed the door behind him, walked a few steps, and then remembered fingerprints. He ran back and wiped the outside doorknob clean. Then he walked down the driveway, trying not to hurry, tossed the bag into his trunk, got into the car and drove off. The rush had finally come.

Thirty-one

Before Donna, the upstairs maid, came into the kitchen, she peeped into the master bedroom and saw that Sally was sleeping soundly. That was about eight-thirty. She vaguely registered the sound of a car starting, thinking that possibly that was Mr. Castle off to the club for golf. The coffeemaker was half full, so Josie must have made coffee and taken a cup either into the study or to the pool-house office. Dickie, as she well knew, having discussed it with Josie the night before, was spending the night in the local jail, and a very good thing she thought it. She would at least have a day without fending off Dickie's pats on her behind or her breasts.

She went to the door and brought in the papers, the *New York Times* and the *Greenwich Time*. Both the *Times* and *Time* were delivered at about seven, but the local paper went to press too early to have anything about Dickie's escapade. Disappointed, she poured a cup of coffee, warmed a croissant, flooded it with butter, and settled down to Ann Landers and then Liz Smith in the local paper.

Donna enjoyed the morning hour. Usually, Sally was not up before nine, and during the week, more often than not, Mr. Castle was off to New York by seven-thirty. It fell on Josie to prepare his coffee, orange juice, and whatever else he might desire. Since this was a Saturday morning, which meant brunch on the terrace instead of a series of breakfasts, Donna had at least an hour to drink her coffee and eat her croissant and read the morning paper in peace. On the other hand, thinking of the blessed absence of Dickie, she concluded that she had been unfair to Mr. Castle in her thinking. He was probably off to the police station to pay Dickie's fine. I don't know why, she said to herself, the way he talks to his father. I'd let him stay there for a day or two. It might do him good.

At nine-thirty, dressed in blue jeans and a T-shirt, Sally came into the kitchen and said to Donna: "Isn't it a perfectly beautiful day! I opened my eyes and I just couldn't think of staying in bed. I feel so worthless when I oversleep, don't you, Donna?"

"My ambition is a whole day in bed."

"Oh, you should be ashamed." Sally would never dare talk to Donna like this if Castle were present.

"With Mr. Right," Donna said, laughing.

"Do you know where Mr. Castle is?"

"I think I heard him take off about an hour ago."

"Then he went to get Dickie, thank God."

"That's what I thought, Mrs. Castle. Do you want some juice and coffee?"

"I'd love it."

"I'll make a fresh pot."

"Don't bother. There's enough left for me, and the kitchen—it's already such a mess. I'm glad Mr. Castle wasn't in here. You know how he hates a mess."

"I know, and if Josie doesn't get in here soon, I'll start." She poured the juice and coffee. Sally took a sip of the or-

ange juice. She could never get used to the pleasure of having fresh-squeezed orange juice waiting for her in the
morning. She disliked ordering the servants to do anything,
but Josie should have been in here, and she said to Donna,
"Please, dear, see if you can find Josie."

"Sure, Mrs. Castle. I'll even go upstairs and look in her
room." Like Josie, she adored Sally, who always said
please, even with the smallest request. Donna wandered
around the house, first to Josie's room and then through the
other rooms and even the basement.

"The only place I haven't looked," she reported to Sally,
"is in the pool-house office. But what would she be doing
there if Mr. Castle has gone downtown?"

"I don't know, but why don't you run out there and see,
please, dear."

A minute later, Sally heard Donna screaming.

Thirty-two

Monsignor Donovan was waiting for Joe Hunt, Abel's son, on the steps of the church that Saturday morning. "I must thank you for allowing me to spoil a beautiful morning. It was good of you to come."

"No problem," Joe said. "A nerd is a nerd. That's my priority."

"I must ask this," Donovan said, somewhat reluctantly, "I must ask that this be in complete confidence. If you can't accept that, then we can't go ahead."

"No problem," Joe repeated. "My lips are sealed."

"Good." He led Joe into the office where the church computer was kept. "What I'd like you to do," Donovan said, "is to find out all you can about Richard Bush Castle. You know—the man who gave the dinner last night. He is, I believe, about sixty-two or -three years old and he's an investment banker with an office in New York. At some

time or another, he had a connection of some sort with the
Jesuits. That's a Catholic order of priests. I'm a Jesuit myself. So you have various paths to follow. I must assure you
that none of this has any malign purpose. He has given our
church a very generous gift, and I must know whether, in
all good conscience, I can accept it. Again, I tell you this in
confidence that you will repeat nothing we find."

"You have my word, Monsignor."

Joe sat down and flicked on the computer. It began to
buzz as they waited, and Joe remarked, "You need a new
model, something state of the art. This is a tired old man."

"But it works?"

"Oh, yes, it works. This will take a few minutes to connect to the Web . . . And here we are, Richard Bush Castle.
No relation to the Bush family. Born in Tedman, Georgia.
Born 1935. Business administration, Berea College, law
degree, Georgetown University, Assistant Secretary of
State 1980–1989 . . . let's try that link. Hmm . . . Not much
more here. Ah, wait . . . Archbishop Oscar Romero, assassinated in March 1980, in San Salvador. Castle was working in the State Department then. I'll try San Salvador."

His fingers laced over the keys. "Wow! Thank God I live
in Greenwich. Six Jesuits murdered in cold blood. Here's a
long statement by Daniel Berrigan. I'll print all of this out
for you. State Department accused. Another statement by
Peter Winch, Workers' Party, and here's Mr. Castle up to
his neck in it. He denies all accusations, calling them utterly absurd and Peter Winch is a liar and his party a com-
munist front. This is part of a long story in the *Washington
Post*. I won't try to read it to you. I'll print it out. I'm putting all of this on a disk, so you have it if you want it."

"Try the Vatican," Donovan said softly.

"The Vatican," Joe repeated. "Whoa! There's enough
here to fill a row of books. Let's see if I can narrow it
down. OK, now here's something. Shall I read it?"

"No. Is it a condemnation?" the monsignor asked
hoarsely. He was standing at the window, gazing across the
churchyard.

"Seems to be."

"Just print it out."

"Eyewitness reports, in the Vatican section."

"I want all of them. Print it."

There were a few seconds of silence as Joe scrolled down the statements.

"Try Honduras, priests—Catholics."

"Two missionary priests missing. Believed murdered by the contras. An Indian woman bears witness. That's a story in the *New York Times*. You want it?"

"Yes, please."

Moments passed, and then Joe said, "Here's Castle again. A hearing by a subcommittee of Congress, Latterbe Johnson, chairman. Castle completely cleared of any involvement in the murder of the Jesuits. A small piece on the back page of the *Washington Post*. I'll print it."

There was no word from the monsignor, standing at the window, his back to Joe.

"I can go on searching," Joe said. "I might be able to find out how this Latterbe Johnson fits in and why he's defending Castle."

"I think I have enough," Donovan said.

"This Castle character's something. When I was at his house last night he seemed like a decent guy. His wife tipped me fifty dollars. But I never knew he was involved in all this Washington business. Don't worry, sir, I'll keep my mouth shut. I'll stick around until we're through printing, just in case the printer goes haywire. You know, sometimes it does."

"Thanks, Joe." Donovan reached into his pocket. "How much do I owe you?"

"Nothing. You pay me for teaching you. This was just an exercise to see how much this old crock could spit out. Not too bad for an old Macintosh. In some ways, they're pretty good."

Thirty-three

Dickie Castle was aggrieved, and not without reason. Here it was, well into the morning, and he was still in the holding cell at the police station, sharing it with a man sound asleep in a drunken stupor.

"Where's my dad?" he yelled. "Where's my breakfast? What are you trying to do, starve me? Hey, somebody!"

A cop appeared with a tray—toast, coffee, jam, and an apple.

"This is my breakfast?" Dickie exclaimed indignantly.

"An apple a day keeps the doctor away. What do you want, Dickie? Steak and potatoes?"

Pointing to the sleeping drunk, Dickie said, "He pissed and shit all over the place. I can't stand the smell."

"My heart goes out to you," the cop said.

"Why can't I wait somewhere else?"

"Because you committed a crime, Dickie. You assaulted

a nice young lady. Anyway, Frank Manelli is coming over here in a little while, and if you were out here, he might just beat the shit out of you before we could stop him." The cop smiled. He knew that Manelli was coming down to drop the charges, but he saw no reason to extend that little bit of comfort to Dickie.

"Fuck you!" Dickie yelled. "Fuck you and fuck Frank Manelli!"

"Someday, Dickie," the cop said, "that mouth of yours is going to get you into a lot of trouble, a lot of trouble."

Thirty-four

Larry drove away from the Castle place with the comfortable feeling that no one had seen him come or go. He was still riding the high of the double killing, with only one worry—that perhaps there had been another copy of the letter. But even if a copy existed—and he did not believe that it did exist—it meant nothing. It was eight forty-five, and by ten o'clock, he would be in his room at the Waldorf. He had left a Do Not Disturb sign on the door.

He had intended to drive to Route 120A and then to 128 south, which would not only take him over the New Croton Reservoir, but would allow him to throw the gun and the ID cards into the water without getting out of the car. Drummond had been very rigid on the matter of getting rid of the gun and cards as soon as possible after the killing, but if he did that, there was the long chance that a cop might stop him for one reason or another. He was in a hurry. He wanted to get back to the Waldorf, and once he had been seen, to take the next shuttle back to Washington. The CIA identification would justify the gun, while with no identification at all, he might well end up in some local jail.

He made his decision and headed for the Round Hill entrance to the Merritt Parkway. He maintained his speed at precisely fifty-five miles per hour, and precisely fifty minutes after he left the Castle pool-house office, he came off the West Side highway, drove to the car-rental garage, wiped his fingerprints off the wheel, and walked to the Waldorf. He congratulated himself. Everything had gone as smooth as silk, and he was a man now with poise and power. He felt newly alive; he was different; he walked differently. He had not given his room key to the desk clerk, and even at this hour of the morning, the great lobby of the Waldorf was crowded. In his light suit, no one noticed him, a tall, well-built man with white hair, an athletic bag slung over his shoulder. There were tall, well-built men with white hair wherever one looked. He remembered that one of the first things he must do in his room was to cut the ID cards into small pieces and flush them down the toilet. He had decided to keep the gun and the ID until the last moment. He would get rid of the gun on his way to the plane.

Then he was at the door to his room. He opened it, and there was Drummond, sitting in the lounge chair, with a gun and silencer on his lap.

"Close the door, Larry," he said.

After the first shock at seeing Drummond, Larry burst out, "How the hell did you get in here?"

"Doors are not an obstacle, Larry. You know that. I came to hear you say, Mission complete."

"What's the gun for?"

"In case it was not you, Larry."

"You can't kill someone in the Waldorf just because they walk into a room. Suppose it was the maid?"

"Why not? It's been done."

"Are you nuts?"

Smiling, Drummond said, "Calm down, Larry. Did you take care of Castle?"

"He's dead."

Raising the pistol—fitted with a silencer, as Larry noted—Drummond said, "So are you, Larry."

"Come on, enough of that, Hugh. You're not going to kill me."

"Why not?"

Larry was terrified. In all his life, he had never been so frightened. His heart was beating wildly, and thoughts were racing through his mind. Should he go for the gun in his jacket pocket? No way to get it out quickly enough. Should he dive at Drummond and take his chances? He was younger than Drummond. If the shot missed him, he could deal with Drummond with his bare hands. But Drummond would not miss. He had practiced pistol shooting at Drummond's place many times. Larry was a good shot, but Drummond was better.

"What sense does it make to kill me?"

"The same sense it made for you to kill Castle. Year two thousand, I'll be governor of my state. That puts you in a position where you can destroy me. I can't live with that hanging over me."

"Why should I destroy you?" Larry asked desperately.

"For the same reason you're clinging to that bag. Castle offered money. You took the money and killed him."

Larry had forgotten that the athletic bag was in his hand. He dropped it now.

"You're a fool, Larry. You'd kill your own mother for money. There's nothing you wouldn't do for money. But you're an asshole. You could have gotten twice what's in that bag if you had played it right. Castle has millions. He'd go on paying for the rest of his life."

At that point, Larry decided to move. He flung himself, not at Drummond, but at an angle, as a football player tackles a man, ripping the gun out of his pocket as he slid across the floor. Drummond's shot tore through Larry's neck, severing the carotid artery, but Larry's shot struck Drummond between the eyes. Larry bled to death, staring at Drummond's dead body.

Thirty-five

Driving from the Greenes' to Stamford, where they intended to inform Nellie's parents of their marital intentions, Nellie asked David, "Why didn't you ever tell me that you were Jewish?"

"Come on, you always knew I was Jewish."

"I knew your father was born Jewish but was some kind of agnostic."

"Lots of Jews are agnostic. It comes with circumcision," David replied, adding, "I'm sorry. That's a smart-ass remark that I rescind."

"OK," Nellie agreed. "But I always heard that Jewish descent goes through the mother. And your mother is a pious Catholic; your sister, too. Your mother said that when you were eleven or twelve, you decided that you were Jewish."

"That's right."

"Does that make you Jewish?" Nellie wondered.

"Why shouldn't it? My mom is a remarkable woman. She never said a word against it. She said, David, if you want to be a Jew, fine. If you ever change your mind, that's all right, too."

"But you were baptized."

"And circumcised."

"So are most of the Christian kids I know."

"Why this sudden interest in religion? I'm as much of a Jew as you are a Catholic."

"But my mother and father are Catholic," Nellie protested.

"But you never go to mass, not even on Christmas. I go to mass on Christmas because the whole family goes. My father goes grudgingly, and he always takes a book with him to read. I think that's pushing it too far, but if my mom isn't annoyed, why should I be? That doesn't make me any more of a Catholic. You're the smartest, most compassionate and beautiful woman in Greenwich—"

"Oh, don't bullshit me like that, David, please!"

"All right, so you're too tall and bony and gawky. Whatever you like."

"That's even more condescending! I ask you a simple question, and all you respond with are smart-ass answers. No, this is not a fight or an argument, and I still love you, and in a few minutes you'll meet my father and mother for the first time—"

"May I interrupt?"

"Sure. Interrupt. Why not?"

"We've been intimate—and I use the word advisedly—for two years now—and loving—"

"Closer to three years," she said.

"Yes, and I adore you, and I'm not a kid, and so help me, God, I'll marry you or stay single all my life, and yet I've never met your parents."

"I thought you understood that. I have my own problems with myself and who I am, Dave. Pull over here by the golf course. We have more to talk about than we can in the three minutes before we reach them."

Obediently, David pulled the car off the road onto the grass swath alongside the fence of Stamford's public golf course.

"OK, here we are."

"You know why you never met my parents. We've talked about it before. Believe it or not, I love you as much or more than you love me. I have since I met you. You were a kid then and you're still a kid, but I figure that in ten years it won't make any difference. There's no rule in this demented country that a wife can't be three years older than her husband, and if necessary you can lie about it and tell my father we're the same age."

"I don't enjoy lying," David said.

"Neither do I, but when it's necessary, I lie. But let me add to what I've said about my parents. My father is a decent, hardworking man, but he's Polish. He was born in 1944. He's a Republican. He hates Clinton and thinks he should be impeached. He hates welfare and thinks people on welfare are worthless bums. He's as reactionary as anyone can be without having a portrait of Hitler on the wall."

"And he doesn't like Jews."

"No, he hates them. Blames them for all the troubles in the world."

"In other words, he's a practicing anti-Semite," David said.

"He doesn't practice it, but he lives with it. I used to argue with him, but then I gave it up. They're pious Catholics. My mother goes to mass every day, and they took it for granted that I would marry into a good Catholic family. They worship the pope, and the one real explosion came about that. I can't bear the pope, with his anti-abortion and his all-male priests and his attitude toward women and all the rest of the garbage, and I said a thing or two that I shouldn't have said. That was when I moved out and went on my own. We've reconciled since then—I'm their only child—but it's a troubled peace."

"And you never told them that my father was Jewish."

Nellie sighed and shook her head. "I simply left it alone. You have red hair and blue eyes and you don't look Jewish."

"Nobody looks Jewish!" David said angrily.

"David, David, don't make this into a fight. My mother dreams of a wedding in a Catholic church. So now, when you tell me that you're Jewish and I fear you'll tell them the same thing—my God, David, I love you. I don't want you in the middle of this disgraceful thing. I kept you away from them until now—not because we're poor and my father is a janitor who lives in a miserable basement apartment, but—well, now you know why."

"About being married—well, I really don't give a damn where we're married, a church or a judge's office. It's being married to you that matters, not how."

"I feel the same way. What should we do?"

They sat in silence for a few minutes, and then a police car pulled up behind them, and the cop got out of the car, walked over to the open driver's window, and asked, "Trouble?"

"Only emotional," Nellie answered, smiling.

"You'll have to work it out somewhere else," the cop said. "Try the mall. No parking here."

He went back to his car, and they drove off. "That's a nice cop," David acknowledged. "He didn't even ask for my license."

David drove through Stamford and into the Ridgeway Mall lot. Looking for an open space, David muttered, "Hail, Mary, full of grace, help me find a parking place."

"I'll be damned!" Nellie exclaimed.

"Credit my sister Claire. She says it always works."

"Does it?"

"I'm afraid not. I have a story to tell you. Can you bear it?"

"I'll try," Nellie said. "How long can we park here?"

"Five or ten minutes should do it. I have a friend up at Harvard, a senior like me. We took two semesters of biology together and got to be good friends. He's from Boston, very Waspy Boston, a very valid Lowell, back to the *Mayflower* and all that. He and his wife live off campus. I met his wife, a lovely black woman, and the next day, I managed to inquire how his folks took it. He asked me to guess, but I couldn't have guessed in a thousand years. You know what his mother said? His mother said, Thank God she's not Jewish."

Nellie stared at him. "True? You're not inventing this?"

"True. Absolutely true. Half a century after the Holocaust."

Nellie spread her hands. "I don't know what to say."

"That manuscript you have in your bag—Harold Sellig's book, *The Assassin*. It's been lying around the house for days. I read an earlier draft of it. It's a book about the Holocaust and Vietnam and the collective guilt of a civilization that he defines by one word, *murder*. He writes that our civilization—not only America but the whole world—is a cult that worships murder. He doesn't admit to civilization; he calls it a sham, even as he calls Christianity a sham along with every other religion, including Judaism. He indicts mankind with the collective guilt of murder. It's one of the most terrifying books I have ever read. He goes into statistics of the twentieth century, the bloodiest century in history, numbers that are appalling. He holds that everyone on earth must share the blame of the Holocaust and Hiroshima and Vietnam. And I tell you, Nellie, that only a Jew could have written this book."

After a time of silence, Nellie said, "Only a Jew? Your mother, your sister, and me? What a terrible indictment you're laying on us! And the Israelis?"

"I'm not an Israeli, I'm a Jew. His list includes Israel. Do you know what this Jewish guilt is? It's the guilt of an outsider who looks at the human race. At least some of us do, and that's the rock bottom of anti-Semitism. They don't want us to observe them, they want us to join, and that's something I'll never do."

Silence again, and they sat in silence for at least ten minutes, a very long time for two people sitting in the front seat of a car in a shopping center; and to both of them, it seemed a good deal longer.

Finally, Nellie said, "I have a suggestion."

"Thank goodness. I don't."

"Let's drive back to Greenwich and out to Tod's Point and find a quiet place along the shore, and we'll sit close to each other and watch the waves and the gulls and hold hands."

David nodded. "What about your father and mother?"

"We'll put that off until we solve it."

"I like that."

"And then," Nellie said, "we can have lunch somewhere."

"I'm broke."

"My treat. And then, after lunch, we can go to my place and make love."

"I like that, too," David agreed. "My father said that during the Vietnam War, there was a tremendous peace movement, and their slogan was, Make love, not war."

Thirty-six

Knowledgeable residents of Greenwich said of the local police department that it was not as bad as its severest critics said it was, but ever since the still unsolved Moxley murder, two decades before, the police had been the butt of constant criticism; nevertheless, Greenwich had its own Criminal Investigation Department, headed by John MacGregor, a fifty-year-old veteran of New York City Homicide. MacGregor had served his time in New York, and he was pleased with his new job in Greenwich, the more so because in twenty years Greenwich had had less than half a dozen murders. He looked upon the town as a good place to live out his years without too much stress.

He happened to be at the police station when a 911 call came in, informing them that a double murder had taken place at the Castle home out in the Back Country. Actually, he was on his way out, and Ginny, the woman at the front desk, caught him at the door.

"Who called it in?"

"An hysterical woman. But it's the Castle place out off North Street."

"Real?"

"Yes, sounds real."

"There are two cars north of the Merritt. Head them over there. Give me the address. And tell Seeber to get his ass out here. Got the address?"

She handed him a paper slip.

"And tell them not to touch anything. Just seal it off."

Cal Seeber appeared, a plainclothes detective in his forties, heavyset, with a perpetual frown.

"Come with me," MacGregor said, handing him the slip of paper. "Do you know where this is?"

"Sure. The Castle place."

"Then, let's go."

Driving across town, from Mason Street and police headquarters to the Back Country, MacGregor said, "I understand we got Castle's son in the cooler and that this Manelli guy has dropped the charges. How long have we had him?"

"Since midnight yesterday. That lets him out."

"Maybe yes, maybe no," MacGregor said. "We got no time yet on the killing."

"Castle was with them when they took the kid away."

"That lets him out."

"Manelli dropped the charges, so we have to let him go."

"I want the kid held until we get back. Or better yet, bring him out to the house. I want to talk to him. What's the kid like?"

Seeber made the call on the car phone.

"Seventeen, eighteen, snotty little bastard," Seeber said. "Rich-kid syndrome. Drives a two-seater BMW. He's a package from Castle's first wife."

"So talk about Castle."

"Very rich, even by Greenwich standards. Big four-million-dollar house. I hear he used to be in the government, Assistant Secretary of something, years ago. Now he's an investment banker. Dumped his first wife and married one of them trophy wives. That's a Greenwich expression for number two or three."

"What's number two like?"

"Like about forty," Seeber went on. "She's a real classy woman. Strawberry blond, even in the roots. And built. I heard she ain't much on the brain side. I went up there once to talk about the kid, when he smashed up his car. She's a weeper, and she turned me over to Castle. He seemed like a decent enough guy, tried to give me a couple of hundred to go easy on the kid. I don't take. But he didn't go into a rage, like some of them do."

"And wife number one?"

"She's in L.A. Drugs, white soldiers. I got an inquiry from L.A. when they arrested her. She's out on parole by now, but it don't look like no woman's job."

"You'd be surprised. When we get there, you call State Forensics and tell them to send down a fingerprint man. Who's in the prowl cars?"

"I think Johnson and Lowsky."

"They'll call an ambulance, won't they?"

"I guess so—if either of the two are alive."

"Trouble with Greenwich," MacGregor said, "is that you don't have enough homicide to establish a routine."

"Maybe it'll improve, Chief, now that you've taken over."

"And I don't like smart-ass, Seeber. I ask; you tell me. Plain?"

"No problem," Seeber replied.

Following Seeber's directions, MacGregor pulled into the driveway of the Castle estate. Seeing nothing moving, he followed the driveway around the house to the pool and pool house, where two police cars were parked, the two uniformed policemen talking with a young, attractive black woman in a maid's dress and apron.

"She found the bodies," one of the uniformed cops, name of Johnson, said to MacGregor.

"Where are the bodies?" MacGregor asked.

Nodding toward the pool house, the other patrolman said, "In there. That's Mr. Castle's office."

"Who?"

"Castle and the downstairs maid. Her name is Josie Brown."

At this, Donna began to weep. The second cop, whose name was Lowsky, put his arm around her and said, "Easy, kid. Just work easy. You'll be all right."

"Either of you touch anything inside?" MacGregor asked the cops.

"No, Chief. Just tried a pulse on the black kid in there. No pulse, she took two in the chest. Castle had his brains shot out."

"Where's the wife?"

"Donna here got her into the house. She's taking it hard, according to this kid."

"Did you call for an ambulance?"

Lowsky nodded.

"From the car phone, I hope. You didn't touch the phone in there," pointing to the office.

"No, Chief."

"OK. Take Donna into the house, and keep her and the wife there. Don't question them. Anyone else around?"

"No one."

MacGregor turned to Johnson: "You drive out to the front, and park so no one else gets in here except the ambulance. Me and Seeber, we'll be inside here or in the house. If her lawyer comes, let him in. Anyone else, come and ask me."

Then MacGregor and Seeber went into Castle's poolhouse office. MacGregor opened and closed the door with his handkerchief. The cops must have done the same. He could see that it was wiped clean. Stepping carefully to avoid the pools of blood, they stood and stared at the bodies.

"She must have come in when the perp had the gun in his hand," Seeber observed. "Fell and slopped the coffee she was carrying."

"He's got blood on his shoe," MacGregor said.

"Might be one of the cops. The computer's on."

"Sometimes, they leave it on. Something about the processor. Go out and call State and tell them to send a computer guy down with the fingerprint man. Not with this phone. Step out and use the car phone."

MacGregor continued to look around him. Except for a large wood and metal desk, the computer, printer, and a facsimile machine, there was nothing there. Not even a picture on the wall. The desk had three drawers on each side and a drawer in the middle and on the desk, there were two glasses, one partly full, and a bottle of scotch. Again using a handkerchief carefully, MacGregor opened the six side-drawers. The middle drawer was locked, he took out a pocketknife and slid the blade in without result, damning the fact that it was a square bolt. The other drawers were empty.

Apparently, it was a very new desk. On its surface, which contained a brass desk set, pen, and letter opener, the desk was smooth, shiny, and empty, except for one uneven spot where the finish was slightly marred. He ran his fingers over the marred spot, and then bent over the desk and smelled the spot. Something had been burned there, he decided. Who burns something on the top of a new, steel-topped desk? A cigar? There was a faint tinge of cigar scent in the room, but this was somehow different. Something had been burned on the desk. A cigar, partly smoked, was on the floor.

Seeber returned. "State doesn't have a computer expert they can send on a Saturday. They say we should find one here or ask Norwalk."

"Screw Norwalk. What do you do when your computer goes haywire?"

"There's a place on Mason Street."

"The hell with that! Is the ambulance on the way?"

"Should be here any minute." Seeber held up a bullet. "It must have gone straight through her. I found it outside the door in the grass."

"Good. Bag it, and we'll send it up to State."

MacGregor's spirits were rising. It was all very well to talk about a peaceful and pleasant retirement, but after twenty-five years of New York City homicides, the peace and quiet of Greenwich had begun to wear on him. He had little imagination for other things than violent death, but within the scope of his experience he was as good as the best. He was a short, stocky man, born in Glasgow; and while his wife would be disturbed by this interruption, he was professionally delighted. Until now, he had dealt with burglaries, a new field and not too engaging. Here, he was at home.

He went through Castle's pockets, hoping he would find the key to the desk drawer. No key. But the killer might have found the key. MacGregor began to crawl around the room on his hands and knees.

"What in hell are you up to?" Seeber asked.

"This!" MacGregor announced, holding up the key. "Right here in the corner. That's where the perp threw it."

MacGregor opened the desk drawer, gave a small leather date book to Seeber, and opened the file. "Go through it page by page," he said. "Find something useful." But how would Seeber know that something was useful? Spreading the papers in the file folder, MacGregor went through them.

He found nothing that appeared to connect.

"I got something," Seeber said.

"Show me."

"It's a date book. Not many entries. He must have another date book, maybe in the house. But here, look, today's date, '250 M to Larry.'"

Seeber rose in MacGregor's estimation.

"Two hundred and fifty grand, that's one hell of a piece of change. Anything else about Larry?"

"No. Want to go through it again?"

"Later."

At that moment, the ambulance arrived. MacGregor took a piece of soft chalk from his pocket. "Draw a line around the bodies. Don't need to be perfect. Just position them." He turned to the two ambulance men, "One of you a doctor?"

"I'm an intern," the younger man said. "What a bloody mess. We don't have anything like this in Greenwich."

"You got it now. Can you give me something about the time of death, Doc?"

"Like in the movies? Well, they were shot this morning. I was never asked that question before," the intern said, as if the question were more important than the grisly scene on the floor. "Maybe two hours ago, maybe more. The room is air-conditioned, so that throws it off."

"You'll do an autopsy?" MacGregor asked.

The intern shrugged. "I don't know. I never been in a situation like this before. Usually, autopsies are only done with permission from, or at the request of, the family. I'll find out at the hospital. Where can I reach you, Officer?"

"At the station house. My name's MacGregor."

"Why didn't you ask him to keep his mouth shut about it? We'll have TV trucks and reporters all over the place," Seeber said.

"We'll have them anyway. Let's go into the house and talk to the ladies, and take the Larry book with you."

The pool was behind the house. Donna let them in at the back door. They walked through a utility room into the kitchen. MacGregor was amazed at the size of the kitchen.

"Where's Mrs. Castle?" MacGregor asked.

"In the living room, lying down on the couch. She's just a wreck, poor thing."

"You like her?"

"She's a sweetheart."

"And Mr. Castle?" MacGregor asked.

"He's all right. He pays Josie and me good money—oh, God forgive me! Poor Josie."

"Take it easy, Donna," MacGregor said. "Sit down."

"I got to bring some coffee to Mrs. Castle."

"In a moment, Donna. Now tell me, how long you been working for the Castles?"

"Six years. Josie got me the job when I graduated from high school. What am I going to tell her momma? Josie's her only child. She lives up in Norwalk. What am I going to tell her?"

"We'll take care of that," MacGregor said gently. "You give her address and telephone to Detective Seeber here. Now Donna, you know of any friend of Mr. Castle whose name is Larry?"

"Larry what?" Donna asked.

"Just Larry."

Donna shook her head.

"All right. You think about that, and maybe you'll remember something. Bring the coffee in, and then come back and give the information about Josie to Detective Seeber."

MacGregor followed Donna into the living room. Sally sat on a couch, her legs tucked under her, her face streaked with weeping, and a box of tissues next to her. Even drawn as her face was with grief, MacGregor saw a beautiful woman. She wore a T-shirt and jeans, her feet bare. MacGregor noticed that her toenails were not painted. During his years on the New York police force, he always noticed fingernails and toenails.

"Please, have some coffee," Donna begged her. "I brought you a hot roll."

Sally shook her head.

"Leave the tray here on the coffee table," MacGregor told Donna, "and go back to the kitchen and talk to Detective Seeber." Then he pulled a small chair up to the couch and said gently, "I'm Captain John MacGregor of the Greenwich police, Mrs. Castle. Do you feel you can talk to me?"

At first, Sally simply stared at him without replying. Then she whispered, "I'll try."

"Good. Thank you. Can you tell me what happened this morning—only what happened to you?"

She took a deep breath, and about a minute passed. MacGregor waited patiently. Finally, Sally whispered, "I woke up, and Richard was up. He almost always gets up first. I put on blue jeans and a T-shirt because I know he likes that and then I went down to the kitchen." She spoke slowly and with effort, and then paused.

"Yes, ma'am."

"I asked Donna to find Josie and she looked through the house. She thought Richard had gone to get Dickie." She paused. "You're a policeman, so you know about Dickie. He's Richard's son," she said, still with each sentence broken.

"I do. Take a deep breath and just tell me what happened."

"I'm trying."

MacGregor nodded. He waited without pressing her.

"I said she might be in his pool-house office. Donna went out to look and I heard her screaming. Then I ran out to the pool house. At first she wouldn't let me in, she's so good to me, like I was her momma. I pushed past her—" She began to cry again, her body wracked with sobs. Mac-Gregor handed her a tissue and waited.

"Richard's dead."

"Yes, ma'am."

"Is Josie dead?"

"Yes."

MacGregor sat and waited until the sobbing stopped. "I must ask you some questions, Mrs. Castle."

"Richard was so good to me."

MacGregor hated to get emotionally involved in a situation like this. It clouded his judgment. "Do you know a man called Larry?"

She looked at him blankly, saying nothing.

"I repeat, do you know a man called Larry?"

"Larry?"

"Yes."

She wiped her eyes. MacGregor offered her the cup of coffee, and she took a sip, spilling some of it on her shirt. MacGregor handed her more tissues and took the cup from her shaking hand. "Yes, he comes here. Sometimes for dinner. Sometimes he comes to talk to Richard and they stay in the study."

"What's his last name?"

She shook her head. "I don't know."

"But if he comes to dinner, you must know."

"Richard called him Larry. That's all. Richard once called him names."

"What names?"

"It was the only time he ever spoke to me about Larry."

MacGregor realized it was the first time she was away from the present moment, and he took advantage of it. "Tell me his exact words, please."

"Do you think he killed Richard?"

"I want to hear the exact words your husband spoke to you."

"Well, something like this: Would you believe that fuckin' son of a bitch was in Congress; no wonder we're in such deep shit. Then Richard told me never to repeat what he said. Now I've broken my promise. I don't talk like that . . . Richard wasn't really talking to me—he was just so angry."

"You helped Richard," MacGregor assured her. "Now, are you absolutely sure he said Congress, not something that sounded like Congress?"

"Yes, Congress. I know what Congress is."

"Where is Richard's study?"

"There," she said, pointing to a door at the end of the room.

"I'd like to look around the study. I don't have a warrant, so I need your permission."

"Will it help?"

"I think so. I also think you should go upstairs to bed, Mrs. Castle. Very soon, there'll be TV crews up here and reporters and a lot of nosy people. We have a policeman and a police car outside, and Detective Seeber will stay here and keep people out, unless you want a doctor or a friend or relative to be with you?"

"I have no relatives," Sally began, and she was going to

add to that, no friends she could call, when she remembered Sister Pat Brody. "Sister Pat Brody at St. Matthew's. If you can reach her, she might come, and maybe you could ask them to let my stepson, Dickie, come home."

Thirty-seven

At about the same time, on this Saturday morning in Greenwich, Ruth and Harold Sellig were at the undertaker's, looking at the face of Dr. Seth Ferguson. Since several parts of his body had been taken from him to help whoever they might help, only his face was visible, and after a minute or so, Ruth turned away. Then they closed the coffin.

"I hate the way we deal with death," she said to Harold.

"Seth isn't here."

"Where is he?"

"That's the big unanswered question, isn't it? You go to sleep, where are you?"

"In my bed, Hal. Don't try to comfort me. Dad is gone."

"Are you sure you want to go through with the cremation?"

"That's what he wanted," Ruth said. "We have no choice."

"He loved your mother. He never looked at another woman."

"Of course he did."

"Well, you know what I mean. Sure, women loved him; everyone did. It doesn't mean we can't bury the ashes next to your mother."

"Hal, how long since you went to your parents' graves?"

"Years."

"I went to my mother's grave once. I went alone. Dad shrugged it off. She's not there, he said. He didn't want to contemplate what the worms left."

"Odd. You know, he wouldn't bait his hook. I had to do it. That's an odd position for a doctor to take."

"He wasn't just a doctor. He was—," Ruth began, but Harold continued.

"He was what a man should be. Unlike you, I've had an intimate acquaintance with death. I saw the body bags in Vietnam lined up as far as you could see."

"Is that supposed to comfort me?"

They were in their car now, and Harold turned to his wife and asked where she wanted to go.

"Could we take out the boat and sail for a while, Hal? I know that's a strange thing to ask. But he loved the boat. He said to me once that he was happy I had married a man of skills, and I asked him what skills he meant, when I always had to help you put a ribbon in your typewriter; and he said to me, He sails a catboat properly. That's a virtuous skill."

"Really? Did he say that?"

"He did."

They had never joined any of the several yacht clubs that lined the Long Island Sound shore of Greenwich. They kept their boat during the winter in the semipublic anchorage at Tod's Point. Summertime, it was anchored offshore at their house, where they had riparian rights. They changed clothes at home, rowed out to their anchorage, climbed into the catboat, and hooked their tiny rowboat onto the buoy. It was almost noon now, and a soft breeze rippled the glowing surface of the sound.

Harold raised the sail, asking whether there was any special place Ruth wanted to go, to which she replied, "Nowhere and everywhere. Just sail."

She had taken her place at the tiller, and he stretched out on the seat, facing her. "By the way," he said, "there was an E-mail for us. The monsignor at the church is going to talk about Seth tomorrow morning. We're invited. Eleven o'clock."

"What church?"

"Saint Matthew's."

"I've never been to a Catholic service. Do you want to go?"

"Whatever you want," Harold assured her.

"Have you ever been?"

"Oh, sure. On the carrier we had a priest and services. We also had a minister and a rabbi. Also onshore. With that much killing around, they wanted to make sure the kids had safe subsequent passage, and don't forget, I was writing a history."

"Which was never published."

"It will be. Right now, it belongs to the navy. I'm suing them for the rights."

"That'll be the day."

"The question is, do you want to go?"

"How do you suppose they know that Dad died?"

"There's a priest at the hospital."

"All right," Ruth said, "I'm in your boat. This is the first moment of peace I have had since Dad died. I don't want to say that I won't go to a Catholic church to hear what a priest says about my father. That would be bigotry. So if you want to go, I'll go with you."

"I do want to go. I had dinner with this priest last night, and the conversation turned to my Greenwich manuscript. The priest hedged his opinion, and a fat little nun there, Sister Brody by name, pushed him about it."

"What did they say?" Ruth asked.

"Oh, I can't really recall all of it, except that he hedged his approval—which was there, nevertheless—but the nun didn't. I haven't asked you, but what changed your mind about the manuscript?"

"I'm not sure I know. Sitting there in the waiting room last night, it was different. Everything was different. You think about what you would do or be if someone close to you, someone you love and depend on, were to die. I think about you in Vietnam, and what my life would be if you didn't come back."

"You wouldn't be awakened by my screams in a nightmare."

"I don't mind being awakened. I can hold you in my arms. It's like holding Oscar in my arms when he was a little boy."

"Yes," he agreed sourly. "You're a good soul, Ruthie. All you photographers think you have to be tough as nails, but you're a sweetheart. I'll try to stop dreaming."

"You can't stop dreaming. But in that waiting room, I had a premonition about Dad. When they took him back to the operating room, I knew it was over. I prayed that it wasn't, but I knew—and I felt perhaps a little bit of what was all around you in Vietnam. Don't Jews believe in an Angel of Death?"

"An Angel of Death, the *Malakh ha-Mavet*. I remember my father speaking about it, and I asked him what kind of an angel represents death, and how can he be an angel?"

"And what did he say, Hal?"

"What he always said about such questions, that someday I'll learn."

"Did you learn?"

"Maybe, maybe not. You know, it's a funny thing, Ruthie, here we are, a Jew and a Presbyterian, and neither of us believes in God, and sometimes in Vietnam I wished there was a God, so I could cuss him out and express my hatred of him and every one of his stinking religions, and

here we are talking about souls and angels. You know—
you know something?—Seth had all our doubts, and when
I said the same thing to him, he said to me, Why, Hal? God
didn't make Vietnam. That was Kennedy and Johnson and
Nixon."

"It was, wasn't it?" Ruth said.

"I guess so."

"We're almost at Long Island. We should tack. Watch
the sail."

Thirty-eight

The cop unlocked the door of the holding cell and said to Dickie, "Come on. You're going home."

"To what do I owe this act of mercy? Did Dad bail me out?"

"Mr. Manelli dropped the charges."

"About time. I didn't hurt that kid. I didn't do anything to her."

"No perp does."

"How do I get home?" Dickie wanted to know. "Do I walk?"

"No, I'll drive you home."

It wasn't until they were in the police car on their way, that the cop told Dickie. "Your father's dead, Dickie."

"My dad's dead? What is this—some kind of dumb joke?"

"He was murdered this morning."

"What! You're crazy. Who'd murder my dad?"

"That's all I know, Dickie, and I can't talk about it. Captain MacGregor's at your home. He'll tell you what you need to know."

"What about Sally?"

"Who's Sally?"

"My dad's wife."

"All I know," the cop said, "is that your dad was shot and that a maid, name of Josie, was shot, both dead. I'm sorry for you, because I know this is a terrible blow, but it's just all I know. So you'll have to wait until I get you home. I wish I could tell you more. But there's a lock on it."

"What does that mean?"

"It means that nobody at the police station can talk about it."

Dickie did not weep. Whatever feeling he had for his father, it was overwhelmed by release. Now he was free. He knew his father was a very rich man, and while he had provoked his dad on various occasions, Castle had never threatened to cut him out of his will. He rubbed his eyes and bent his head. He didn't want the cop to report that he had no feelings at all, surprised himself at how little grief he had. He had spent much of the night in the holding cell thinking of how little concern his dad had for him. Well, his dad was gone, and it was none of his doing. It never occurred to him that he was a psychopath, because he hadn't the slightest notion of what a psychopath was, or that he felt no guilt or was incapable of feeling guilt. He had often wished his father dead, and here it had happened. It wasn't, he thought, like his father dying of a heart attack. They'd blame him for that. They always blamed him. The only problem was that bitch, Sally. Why wasn't she included? Suppose his dad had left everything to her? That thought disturbed him.

Meanwhile, sliding over the mysterious paths that information takes, news had spread, and as both noon and the car carrying Dickie approached, two TV trucks and assorted newspaper reporters and curious onlookers had gathered, full of frustration, at the entrance to the Castle driveway. An enterprising reporter had even climbed the stone wall that stretched away on either side of the driveway and had approached the door of the house, only to be hustled back to the gates by Detective Seeber.

There was good reason for these tight precautions. Sitting in Castle's study at his burnished mahogany desk, MacGregor had picked up Castle's telephone and asked the operator to connect him with the chief of the New York City office of the FBI. After claiming police privilege to several connections and several phone patches, he found himself talking to Agent Frederick Gunhill.

MacGregor identified himself, specifying his long background with New York P.D. as a homicide detective, and after MacGregor gave his social security number, date of birth, and his mother's maiden name, Gunhill was ready to listen.

"Here's what we have," MacGregor said. "This morning, about eight-fifteen or so, two people were shot to death on the estate of Richard Bush Castle, here in Greenwich, Connecticut. One of them was Castle himself, and the other was a housemaid, name of Josie Brown. I arrived at the scene of the crime an hour and a half ago. I made a first cursory examination of the scene, spoke to a second woman employed here as a maid, and then to Sally Castle, wife of the deceased. Meanwhile, going through Castle's date book, I found a notation for this morning. The name Larry, no surname, along with two-five-zero M. As I understand, M for thousands."

"You're talking about two hundred and fifty thousand cash?" Gunhill interrupted.

"Possibly. I have his checkbook in front of me. No two-fifty M. The last check is ten thousand, made out to St. Matthew's Church, here in Greenwich."

"Go on, Captain."

"I questioned Mrs. Castle. Not as a suspect, I'm sure of that. She recognized the name Larry, but didn't know the surname. She identified him as a frequent visitor and alluded to the fact that her husband had mentioned him as a former congressman."

"Hold on here," Gunhill said. "Before we go any further, I must specify that you are to give out no information—none at all. Do you understand me?"

"I understand."

"Two people have been brutally killed by a criminal intruder. You have no leads, no fingerprints, no evidence whatsoever. Has anyone spoke to Mrs. Castle?"

"Just myself and my assistant, Detective Seeber."

"Was he witness to your questioning of Mrs. Castle?"

"No, sir. I was alone with her."

"Where is she now?"

"I'm calling from Castle's study in his house. She is upstairs in her bedroom, in bed I presume. She was terribly shaken."

"Reporters? Television?"

"There are two TV trucks outside the estate gate, Cablevision and a CBS truck. Several reporters. I gave strict orders for the driveway to be blocked and neither Mrs. Castle nor the maid to speak to anyone."

"That was very intelligent of you, MacGregor. What were your reasons?"

"The mention of a congressman. That's why I called you."

"Thank God," Gunhill said. "This is very explosive. In your discussion with Mrs. Castle, did she ever mention Latterbe as a first name, or Latterbe Johnson as a full name?"

"No, sir. But I've read that name somewhere."

"I'm sure you have," Gunhill said. "This is the most delicate matter I ever encountered in all my life as a federal agent. I've already been in touch with Washington. Now I must give you some facts, MacGregor, and from what you tell me, I think you're a good enough American to sit on them—for the rest of your life, if need be. Larry once was

Congressman Latterbe Johnson. We still have a good deal of investigating to do, but it's pretty clear in my mind, from what you have told me, that he killed Castle and the housemaid. That doesn't mean you drop the investigation. It must continue until it's locked away as a dead file. Now how long will it take me to get to Greenwich?"

"From downtown New York? Well, there shouldn't be much traffic today. An hour, perhaps."

"I'll be there—oh, say two hours. Nobody talks to Mrs. Castle."

"Well, sir," MacGregor said uneasily, "she asked whether a local nun, Brody by name, could come to see her. I agreed. She desperately needs someone."

"Are the Castles Catholic?"

"I don't think so. No signs of it anywhere in the house. Except for the check to St. Matthew's."

"All right. Let the nun in. You might mention to Mrs. Castle that Larry is an old friend of Castle's who might be hurt if you mentioned his name as a suspect."

"I understand."

"I'll see you later. I want you to remain there, at the house."

It was only after MacGregor hung up and saw the patrol car bringing Dickie home that he recalled with chagrin that he had not mentioned Castle's son.

He resisted the impulse to call Gunhill again. He'd have to handle Dickie very gingerly, and he intercepted him as Dickie entered the house with Seeber.

"How're you taking it, kid?" MacGregor asked him.

"I got to take it. It's a rotten break. I loved my father." No tears, no breaking voice. "Do you know who killed him?"

"Not yet, but we're moving on it. I got the whole force moving on it."

Seeber raised a brow and then frowned. But he usually frowned. "Chief," Seeber said, "you got to go out there and make a statement. We can't keep putting them off."

"In a moment. I want a word with Dickie here first." He

drew Dickie off to one side, put a friendly hand on his shoulder and said, "You're carrying a big load now, son, and I don't think your mom is up to it."

"She's not my mom," Dickie said.

This stupid little bastard, MacGregor said to himself, feeling that somehow he had to win the boy's trust. "I understand. I can imagine how your real mom must feel. We'll have to notify her. You must tell me where I can reach her."

"I don't know where she is. Somewhere in California."

"Who would know?"

"Jim Cartwright, Dad's lawyer. He sends out her checks every month. Dad always squawks about it, but he sends them out, and Dad signs them."

Doesn't this kid realize his father's dead? MacGregor wondered. "You got things to do, son. You have to face up to it."

"Yeah. When will his will be read?"

MacGregor sighed. "That's up to Mr. Cartwright. Meanwhile, two people are dead. I'll be talking to Josie's parents, but you got to go to the hospital and get the death certificate and arrange for the funeral."

"Can't someone else do that? I don't know how to arrange a funeral. I never had anyone die on me before."

"Do you know where Cartwright's office is?"

"Yeah, on Mason Street."

"Well, why don't you go into your father's study and call Mr. Cartwright. I think he'll take all these details off your hands."

Dickie stared at MacGregor for a moment or two, then he nodded and went into his father's study. MacGregor turned to Seeber. "You been listening?"

"I been listening. If that was my kid, I'd boot him from here to Alaska."

"He's not your kid, Cal, so relax. We're in the middle of a piece of bad monkey business. I know who killed Castle, and I can't tell you or anybody else."

"For God's sake, who?"

"No way, and we're not going to find the killer. But we have to put on a show and leave no stone unturned trying to find him. This afternoon, two federal agents are going to show up here."

"Chief, if you can't trust me—"

"I trust you, Cal. I'd trust you with my life. But that's the way the feds want to play it, and if I'm guessing right, they're going to wipe out any connection between the perp and Castle. That poor black woman was a mistake. She got in the way."

Dickie came out of his father's study now. "Mr. Cartwright says to come right over. He didn't even know about my dad being dead. It was a big shock to him. He says I should come right over and he'll take care of everything. He's got Dad's will in his safe." And without taking a breath, "Who do you think killed my dad?"

"We'll find him. I think it was someone intending to rob him, and when he saw your dad go into the office outside, he followed him. Then Josie walked in on them by mistake, and he started shooting." Seeber nodded. It was as good an explanation as any.

"Can I drive?" Dickie asked. "I mean my own car?"

"Sure. I'll ride up to the gate with you," replied Mac-Gregor, thinking, *and deliver my line of bullshit to the eager audience.*

Thirty-nine

Sister Brody was driving out to the Castle home, in response to Sally's tearful, pleading telephone call. Sister Brody was also in the midst of a perplexing ethical battle with herself. This was not a frequent state of mind for Sister Brody. Usually, she knew what to do, and she did it. She had served in El Salvador, Nicaragua, Guatemala, and Honduras; and now the church was giving her a much-needed reprieve in Greenwich.

She had accepted the post in Greenwich because she felt she had given in to a surfeit of anger. She had always fought with all her soul to resist anger. To her, controlling and understanding anger was a part of her work; uncontrolled anger was a sin, even when the anger was turned by herself against herself; and after all that she had seen and been a part of, Greenwich was an island of peace and quiet. Nevertheless, driving out to the Back Country, she faced what was perhaps the most vexing ethical problem she had encountered in years. It concerned Sally Castle.

Sister Brody loved her church and believed wholly in its tenets. Death saddened her enormously, yet she believed fervently that it was simply a transition to another state. She had been a part of long discussions with people who believed otherwise, yet her belief had not been shaken.

Her church was her mother and father and lover, yet she disagreed politically with major parts of the Catholic Church. In her political ideas she was totally a follower and supporter of the Berrigan brothers, and she had once argued with Monsignor Donovan that if a miracle occurred and Father Daniel Berrigan became the next pope, all the working billions of the world would join the church, to which the monsignor replied that miracles were infrequent and that time itself was a miracle more dependable than daydreams.

Her response, not to the monsignor but to herself, was that the monsignor had spent so much time in meditation that he was beginning to think like a Zen roshi.

Still and all, here was the problem she faced and was trying to solve during the forty minutes it took to drive from St. Matthew's to the Castle home. She knew that the Catholic Church was both the wealthiest and the poorest in the world. The treasures in the Vatican were valued at untold billions, yet every active priest and nun was, in fact, a beggar. No matter how much money St. Matthew's had, they were always in debt. When the thought entered her mind that neither the pope nor any cardinal had ever missed a meal, she prayed for forgiveness for even entertaining the idea. She had prayed for the souls of Josie Brown and Richard Castle and asked forgiveness for both of them.

She was a keen judge of character, and from her own session with Sally Castle and from what she had observed at the dinner table and afterward, she believed that Richard Castle had loved his wife. Whether he loved her more or less than he loved money was not hers to decide, but she also knew that word around was that he gave little or nothing to charity. Word was also around that he was enormously wealthy and Sister Brody's guess was that he would leave a substantial amount of it to his wife. There was also no doubt in her mind that if she, Sister Brody, used even modest persuasion, Sally would be baptized a Catholic. The question of Sally's openness to acts of charity did not even enter Sister Brody's mind. Sally was an innocent. Innocents formed a definite category of humanity in Sister Brody's mind. She had met many of them in her time, in various countries, people of various races and varied degrees of education. She had seen innocence in physicians, in college professors, in thieves, and in whores. Innocents came in all colors and in all religions, and they were imbued with something beyond her understanding.

Thus her ethical problem. She belonged to a missionary order of the church, and she had been prepared to bring Sally to the Catholic Church regardless of what her husband felt. Now her husband was dead, and Sally would likely become a very wealthy woman, possibly, in terms of St. Matthew's, the wealthiest member of the congregation. How does this influence me, Sister Brody asked herself? Does this make Sally a prize instead of a soul in torment? Am I doing this to influence Sally's newfound wealth, or am I a woman responding to another woman's grief?

She arrived at the Castle estate with the question unanswered. "Help me, please," she whispered.

Captain MacGregor was talking to the media when she arrived and parked in front of the gate.

"As I told you, at this moment we have absolutely no leads, no suspects, but we expect results when the state forensic people arrive. Mrs. Castle is totally devastated by what has happened and will give no interviews. I am keeping the entire place off-limits because those are her instructions. The Greenwich police will not fail the people of Greenwich this time. We will find the perpetrators of this awful crime. This will not be another Moxley case."

A policeman approached Sister Brody's car. "You can't park here, ma'am."

"I'm Sister Brody," she said. "Mrs. Castle is expecting me."

Detective Seeber drove with Sister Brody up the driveway to the house. "You're the only one she asked for, Sister, not even her lawyer. Captain MacGregor doesn't like those scenes where the TV camera is poking into the faces of the bereaved. She says she doesn't want to talk to anyone but you—that's the way it is."

"That's very thoughtful of Captain MacGregor. Please thank him for me," Sister Brody said.

Donna opened the door for Sister Brody, and Seeber went back to the gate. Donna was still very upset, telling the nun that she had been talking to Josie Brown's mother.

"It's so hard to talk to someone with such a loss. How can you explain it? Josie never bothered anyone."

"You must pray for her." What else can I say? Sister Brody wondered. She had faced this question of useless and meaningless murder many times before, and there was no answer to the question.

"How is Mrs. Castle?"

"She's upstairs in her bedroom. I brought her a tray of sandwiches and milk, but she wouldn't touch it."

"What do you do when the telephone rings?"

It was ringing now. Donna shrugged. "Captain MacGregor was here until half an hour ago. He said he'd be back. I let it ring, and the machine answers."

"And where's the boy, Dickie?"

"He went to talk with Mr. Castle's lawyer." Then Donna told the nun about Dickie's night in jail.

"Doesn't he want to be with Sally?"

"They don't get along too well. She tries. But he—"

"I understand. I'll go up to her now."

"I'm glad you're here," Donna said. "It's spooky here with no one except the cops."

Sister Brody climbed the broad staircase to the upper floor.

The door to the bedroom was open, and Sally was seated on a small Queen Anne chair, her hands clasped in her lap. She rose as Sister Brody entered and went to her and kissed her on the cheek. She was still wearing the blue jeans and the T-shirt she had put on this morning. Her hair was tied in a knot at the back of her head, and her eyes were bloodshot from weeping.

"Thank you for coming, Sister Pat," Sally said, almost formally, as if she were practicing to have each word correct. "It was very good of you. Please sit down," indicating another chair. "You said yesterday that I could call you Sister Pat?" she said uncertainly.

"Or Pat, whichever you wish."

"I never had a sister—or a brother."

"That's a shame, isn't it? I'm sure you would have loved sisters and brothers. I have two brothers and a sister."

"Are they like you?" Sally asked.

"They're not as fat as I am," the little nun said, laughing.

"You're not fat."

"Bless you."

"I meant, do they work for the church, like you do?"

"No, Sally. My sister is married and has three children. One brother is a therapist and the other is still in college, still trying to get his Ph.D."

"A therapist?"

"He works with people who are disturbed and need help."

"Oh, I get disturbed."

"We all do at times."

Sally nodded. "At times like today. It's been a terrible day."

"I know."

"I'm better because I knew you'd come."

"I'm happy to be here with you," Sister Brody said.

"Thank you. The policeman, Mr. MacGregor, asked me did I want to call any friends or relatives, but I have no relatives and except for you and Ruth Sellig, I have no friends. Muffy, who was here last night, always pretends to be my friend. She wants to sleep with Richard, and she thinks I'm too stupid to see it. A lot of the women think I'm stupid because I don't play cards or golf or tennis and, I guess, the way their husbands look at me. That's why I don't use makeup or paint my nails, because Richard once said women use them as come-ons. And I hardly ever talk. I read. I only got to seventh grade, but I read a lot. Richard preferred television— Oh, my goodness, I never talked so much before."

"I want you to talk," Sister Brody told her. "And you're not stupid."

"That's what Ruth Sellig says. She's a photographer, not with dirty pictures but faces for magazines and covers. She's Harold Sellig's wife. I invited both of them, but her father was having an operation, so she couldn't come."

"Yes, I know. Her father passed away last night."

Sally's face contracted with pain. "Dr. Ferguson. Oh, I'm so sorry! He was a dear man." Tears came to her eyes. She reached for a tissue and wiped away the tears. "I'm frightened of death, and today has been full of death. Could I ask you a kind of personal question, Sister Pat?"

"Of course."

"I had pneumonia last winter. That's when I met Dr. Ferguson, at the hospital. I had a very high temperature and I thought I was going to die, and I asked him."

"But you didn't die. You got better."

"Yes," Sally said. "But I'm afraid, and that's what I want to ask you. What happens to people who die?"

"I don't know, my dear."

"But you're a nun. Aren't you supposed to know?"

"I have my faith, and my faith tells me that God loves people, that we are his children, and that if we live good lives, we exist in another form after death."

Sally shook her head. "I saw Richard this morning, lying there in his office in a pool of blood with his head smashed. It was the worst thing I had ever seen. How can I think he was alive or will be alive again? I want to, but I can't."

"Did you love him, Sally?"

"That's the funny thing. I don't know if I did or not. I was a little afraid of him. My first husband beat me up, and I had to go to the hospital. My second husband never spoke to me. He showed me off, and then in bed he'd go at me. Richard was the first man who ever treated me decently. He never hit me. He bought me all kinds of things that I didn't even ask for, and he got into a real fight at the club with a man who called me a trophy wife. I wasn't a trophy wife. Richard had left his first wife years before I met him in Los Angeles. But now he's dead and gone forever."

"Can I tell you a little story?" Sister Brody asked.

Sally nodded, and Sister Brody went on, "When I was a little girl, nine or ten years old, I asked my mother what would happen to me if I died. We weren't a Catholic family. I joined the church years later, but that's another story. This time, when I asked her that question, she took a glass of water and a box of salt. Then she put a spoonful of salt on a spoon. Do you see the salt and the water? she asked me. I said I did. Then she poured the salt from the spoon into the water and mixed it well. Where's the salt, Pat? she asked me. You put it into the water, I said; and she said, Do you see it? No, I said. But you saw me put it in, so you know the salt is there. I had to agree to that.

"Well, Sally, you know the salt was still there. But it had changed its form, and suddenly I realized what my mother was saying to me. Only the form of the salt had changed."

Sally had listened to the story intently, her brow furrowed, and after Sister Brody had finished, Sally was silent for a long moment, and then, almost shyly, she smiled.

A beautiful smile, Sister Brody decided, wondering whether she, as a child, had smiled that same way when she first heard this explanation from her mother.

"It's only a story, Sally. But sometimes a story can open a whole new way of thinking."

"I know."

They sat in silence for a little while, Sister Brody debating whether she should open the question of baptism once again. Sally had displayed no sense of being the heir to Castle's fortune. Now, very hesitantly, she asked Sister Brody, "Can I come to your church tomorrow?"

"Of course."

"When shall I come?"

"There's a mass at eleven o'clock in the morning, where Monsignor Donovan will deliver the homily."

"What is a homily?"

"A sermon, more or less."

"Oh, yes. I understand." Sally hesitated.

Misunderstanding her hesitation, Sister Brody assured her that she would be under no obligation if she came. "Anyone can come, Sally. You don't have to be Catholic."

"I know. It's something else, but I've taken so much of your time already."

"I have all the time in the world."

"Well, you know, now I have a lot of money. Richard told me that most of his estate would belong to me after his death, except for a trust fund for Dickie. He was very rich. Now I'm all alone in this big house, and when Dickie has his trust fund, he'll take off. He wants that desperately, and he talks about it all the time. I don't want all that money or this big house. I want to help people who don't have money or food. Will you be my friend? Will you help me with the money?"

"I will always be your friend," Sister Brody said, putting the accent on the word *always*. "But as for the money, you are a mature woman, Sally. You have a lawyer. You will know what to do with your money—all in good time."

Driving back to the church, Sister Brody sighed, thinking, Maybe I did it right, maybe not. I think I was right.

Forty

It was four o'clock in the afternoon when FBI Agent Gunhill arrived at the Castle place, and with him was a Mr. Frillbee, of the Justice Department. Gunhill was a tall, gaunt man who appeared to see nothing in the world as amusing or odd. He was in his forties, Frillbee a decade older. Both wore suits of light twill and Panama-type straw hats. MacGregor introduced them to Sally, and both of them expressed formal regrets for the death of her husband.

"We'd like the use of your husband's study for the next hour or so," MacGregor said, explaining, "There are certain matters of his work in Washington that we must clear up."

"Of course. I can give you coffee and sandwiches."

"That won't be necessary," MacGregor said. "Very kind of you."

"If you should change your mind, there's a hot and cold beverage dispenser in his study."

"Thank you."

Once seated in the study, Frillbee observed, "Castle lived well."

"State of the art in this part of Greenwich," MacGregor said.

"She's a beauty," Gunhill said. His accusatory stare at Sally might have been beyond his control, MacGregor decided.

"What does she know?" Frillbee asked.

"Nothing, as far as I can determine. I pulled out of her the memory of once having heard Castle refer to Larry, as he called him, as a congressman."

"That's disturbing."

A cold chill came over MacGregor. Frillbee's round face reminded the policeman of Kenneth Starr.

"I hear you were a homicide lieutenant with the NYPD."

MacGregor could have said that it was long enough to see everything in the way of dirt and deceit and corruption that any human being could see anywhere, but instead he simply replied, "I served my time and did my job and took my pension."

Frillbee did most of the talking. "And now you are CID in Greenwich?"

"It's a quiet place."

"We checked you out. You have a good record. Why didn't you make captain?"

"I didn't take," MacGregor said.

"Never?"

MacGregor shrugged. "I don't want to sound saintly. I just covered my ass the only way I knew. I didn't take."

"Do you know what we're up against?"

"Some. I can make some guesses. I'd rather hear it from you."

"All right. Larry was the nickname of Latterbe Johnson. Evidently, he drove up here this morning to talk with Castle. Whether something went wrong in their talk or whether it was his plan all along or whether it was the result of being interrupted by the black woman, we don't know. Probably, we'll never know. However, this much we do know, that subpoenas have been issued for three men by a congressional subcommittee of the House, investigating the murder of six Jesuit priests and a Catholic bishop in El Salvador. It was a very dirty business. Castle's subpoena was to be served this afternoon. The two other subpoenas have been served in Washington, or service was attempted, I must say. They were to be served to Larry and a man named Hugh Drummond.

"Yesterday, Larry—we'll call him that—rented a suite in the Waldorf in New York. Drummond joined him there sometime today. Larry rented a car at seven this morning, with the identification of a CIA operative, stolen identification. Evidently, Larry had visited Castle a number of times in the past, and he had given Larry money. This time, Larry came away with a quarter of a million in cash. When Larry returned he met with Drummond at the Waldorf suite. They got into an argument, and they're both dead. As if that were not enough complication, Drummond, a former chief of staff at the White House and a powerful lawyer in Washington, had just announced his candidacy for governor of his state. So that's what we have—three subpoenas, three killings."

The slightest of smiles crossed MacGregor's lips. "I thought I had seen everything," MacGregor said softly.

"Nobody's seen everything, MacGregor. We have a pile of dirt at the worst possible time, with Clinton up to his neck in shit with his women. We had to make quick decisions. Drummond's body is on the way to Washington, and we have an undertaker there who'll cooperate.

"He died of a heart attack. Larry was shot by an intruder. It sliced his carotid artery, so there's enough blood to cover Drummond's bleeding. But the way it stands, the ball is in your court."

And MacGregor thought, If I go along? I have a good wife, I have three kids, I have two grandchildren, and what happens if I don't go along? There are no more heroes. I paid my dues.

"And what are you asking for?"

"An open-end investigation. No perp. Some lunatic walked into that pool house and shot both of them. A simple robbery. Castle kept money in his pool-house office. Cash. Just a simple robbery, an investigation that goes on for a couple of years and then just fades away. You'll be doing a service to your country. If you need money—"

His thought was, Fuck you—both of you bastards!

But he said, "I go along with you—with one caveat." MacGregor liked the word. A cop was supposed to be ignorant.

"What's that?"

"I'll take care of this end, and since you've been through my record, you know my word is good. Nothing happens to Castle's wife, Sally."

"And if she talks?"

"I'll take care of that. She won't talk."

The two government men looked at each other, and then Frillbee nodded. "We'll shake hands on that," he said, wrinkling his lips thinly.

MacGregor responded to Frillbee's wrinkled lips. "Let me put it plainly," MacGregor said. "I don't like this stinking dance of death, but I'll go along every step of the way. But if Sally Castle dies, accident or otherwise, I'll blow this whole pot of bullshit to hell. Is that understood?"

There was a long moment of silence, and then Frillbee said shortly, "Understood."

Forty-one

Unexpectedly, early on Saturday, Muffy's husband had returned from Brazil, and by noon, word of Castle's death was seeping through the Back Country of Greenwich. While Muffy was disappointed by the early and somewhat unexpected return of her husband, it was not an entirely unfavorable event. She shed no tears for Castle's death, but the only tears Muffy had shed since her marriage began were tears of utter frustration.

Her husband was five years older than Castle, and his libido had long been replaced by a fruitless lust for money. His earnings came to some two hundred thousand dollars a year, but with three children in good colleges, he was always in debt. He managed to pay the installments on the huge mortgage he carried on his house, but after leasing his two Mercedes, there was never enough money left to make a month in the black. He was an investment banker, as were so many of his neighbors, but he had neither the brains nor the personality of Richard Castle. The result was a sour and unhappy man.

Muffy loved the casual manner in which Castle had slipped her two or three hundred dollars after each tryst in New York or in her house when she was alone in her house, which was often enough. She knew that money was meaningless to Castle and that he could have had any number of younger and more attractive women had he so desired. She had gone through a face-lift, a tummy tuck, and two buttock tucks; and she had decided that her large, bony frame gave him something that his pretty wife did not provide. He had paid for all of these operations without a quiver or a retort, which made Muffy feel that she was something more in his life than an expensive hooker, even though once he had ejaculated he got out of her house in a quick fifteen minutes. Her husband, Matt, was too absorbed in his own problems to question her story that the surgery was paid for by their medical policy. She kept the records.

But Castle was gone, and Muffy was here, and she was never one to weep over spilled milk. The game had changed, but the substance was still there. Muffy was a good cook. Tonight she prepared her husband's favorite dinner, a delicately roasted standing rib of beef, pink in the center, scalloped potatoes and tiny garden peas, and a bottle of good Merlot. The truth of their relationship was that Matt valued her, and he had neither the will nor the money to start afresh with a new wife; and Muffy was good-looking, if not beautiful. If he suspected her dalliance with Castle, he simply put it out of his mind. She was two inches taller than her husband, and he no longer regarded her as a sexual object.

At dinner that Saturday night, they spoke about the night before, and Matt echoed her surprise at the presence of the two Catholic clerics. "That's crazy," Matt said. "They're not Catholic. Why the hell would they have a couple of priests?"

"The woman's a nun, Matt," she gently corrected him.

"Still the same. Do you suppose Sally's going Catholic?"

"That's something I want to discuss with you. Richard was worth well over two hundred million."

"You're sure?"

"Of course, I'm sure," Muffy replied, feeling no need to explain why she felt so sure. When it came to their circle of acquaintants, Matt always took her word about wealth and marriage and similar matters.

"And he took home better than two million—that's right, two million—out of his work."

"Not where he's going," Matt said, a note of triumph in his voice.

"Yes, he's dead, poor man. I hear the thug who did it shot away most of his head. But right now, Matt, that idiot wife of his stands to inherit almost all of what he had."

"You're kidding."

"I don't kid about such things," Muffy assured him.

"And what about Dickie?"

"The way I heard, Dickie gets a twenty-million-dollar trust fund, which should yield him at least a few hundred thousand in yearly income, which is plenty for that brat. Sally gets the rest. Can you imagine—that stupid, worthless Valley Girl with that kind of money!"

Matt did not ask Muffy how she knew the details of Castle's bequests; he simply accepted it as part of her knowledge of what so many people in the Back Country had and what they spent.

"That's very nice money," Matt admitted.

"That's all you have to say?"

"What else?" Matt wondered.

"If I put a pot of gold in front of you, would you have enough sense to pick it up?" she demanded, barely able to keep the contempt out of her voice.

"Come on," Matt said. "I'm tired. Don't go into one of your tirades about my being poor."

"All right, honey. I know how hard you work. But what does Sally do with that money? She doesn't know a stock from a bond. She can't handle this alone. She has to have a financial advisor, and from what I hear, a good financial advisor can get as much as five percent. Think about that."

The Merlot was gone, and Muffy went to the bar to open another bottle. When she returned and poured the wine, Matt's face had lit up. "Why not?" he said. "Why not indeed? I've known Richard for a dozen years. He was always very decent to me. Sally always seemed to like us—as much as you could ever tell what that dumb broad was thinking. She once asked me what a trust was. She thought it meant that you trusted someone. Are you sure Richard didn't put most of it in trust for Sally?"

"He always intended to, but he was too busy making it. He once said, Let it grow. But I'm not worried about that. What's our next step? What do we do?"

"Have you spoken to Sally yet?"

"No. I was waiting. I was trying to think of the best approach."

"There is no best approach, baby. Just call her right now and tell her how our hearts go out to her. Tell her we're her friends, her close friends. Tell her that we're ready to do anything for her. Invite her to dinner. She can't fry an egg and she knows what a good cook you are. Tell her you'll give her free cooking lessons. Tell her—"

"Matt, don't run away with it!" Muffy said sharply. "I know what to say to her."

"Don't talk about money."

"Of course not. I'm not stupid."

They went into the living room, each with a glass of wine to celebrate action. Matt sipped his wine. Muffy dialed Sally's number.

"My dear, my dear, poor, suffering Sally. How my heart goes out to you! Matt came home today, and we were both in tears . . . Yes, what a loss, what a terrible loss. We want you to come for dinner tomorrow, you mustn't be alone."

At the Castle home, Sally listened to this. When she made no reply, Muffy went on speaking. Still silence. Then, at last, Sally took a deep breath and said, "Thank you, Muffy. Thank Matt. He has a good heart." Once again, Sally took a long pause and said, "As for eating in your house, Muffy, I would die of starvation first, and something else, Muffy"—Sally's voice rose to an ear-splitting shout—"Muffy, fuck you!"

Then Sally put down the telephone and whispered, "God forgive me. I promised you, Richard, that I would never use those words again, but I didn't know what else to say."

Muffy put down the telephone and turned slowly to her husband.

"Did I hear her say fuck you?" he asked. Muffy stared at him without replying.

"Will you goddamn answer me! Did I hear her say fuck you?"

"Yes, Matt, that's what the little bitch said."

"How long have you been fucking Richard Castle?"

"Just watch your tongue, Matt."

"How long!"

"Drop dead, Matt."

"It's over now! It's finally over!" He rose, walked to her, and flung what was left in his wineglass in her face. Then he raised his right hand to strike her. Muffy caught his wrist and snapped, "Don't try that, Matt, or I'll break your goddamn arm. I'm no candidate for a battered wife." Then she pushed him away. "You dumb bastard, Richard would have left me millions. He was just waiting for you to drink yourself to death."

Matt staggered a bit, almost fell, and then pulled himself upright. Swaying with forlorn dignity, he walked out of the house and into the cool June night.

Forty-two

Sister Brody tapped at the door of the monsignor's study. "Come in," he said. She barely heard his voice, but she was sure he said to come in. His door was never locked.

For Sister Brody, who was of Irish people herself, blue eyes and light hair, the expression "black Irish" had a specific meaning. She had always felt that they were different, of a more ancient earth-rooted race, with their lean faces and dark eyes and black hair. Donovan was black Irish—moody, turned in upon himself, lean to the point of emaciation, yet he ate well and had great energy. Through all that she had witnessed during her years of service, she had maintained a certain gaiety, as if she contained a spirit that could surmount any horror. Donovan was different, and that perhaps was why, working at the same church, they were drawn together. She approached him without the reverence that the other church workers showed him. If she were not a nun, she might have admitted to herself that she was in love with him, but she was a nun and well past forty, and so to some degree she mothered him and he turned to her and sometimes spoke to her of things he left unspoken in confession.

"I drove out to see Sally Castle. I spent an hour with her," the nun said.

"Yes. How is she taking all this?"

Sister Brody dropped into a chair beside the monsignor's desk.

He sat behind the desk, which was piled with books and papers, leaving room only for a small crucifix.

Sister Brody shook her head. "I don't know. She appeared to be unusually calm. I don't know what was between her and her husband."

"That's something almost impossible to know about any couple, isn't it?"

"I suppose so," Sister Brody agreed. "Anyway, she's coming to church tomorrow morning for the eleven o'clock mass to hear you speak."

"Oh? So that's why you're here."

"Yes—I suppose."

"How do you know?" Donovan asked without rancor.

"I saw the bulletin in the office. It says that Father Garibaldi will deliver the homily."

"Yes, word does get around. Is that so disappointing?"

"It will be to Sally and to the Greenes and the Selligs as well. They will all be here; but Sally, must I greet her with a lie?"

"It's not a lie."

"It's my lie. I told her you would speak about the three people who died today and last night," the nun insisted.

"I can't. It's impossible."

"May I ask why it's impossible?"

No one else at the church would have dared to beard him like that, yet he didn't tell her that it was none of her busi-

ness or ask her to leave. Sister Brody guessed that he
wanted to talk. She waited quietly while the silence thick-
ened and became more difficult.

"Pat," he finally said, almost pleadingly, "would you
mind if I smoked? I know it's a disgusting habit, and I've
tried to break myself of it—I know, last night, but that was
a Cuban cigar—"

She couldn't help herself. She began to giggle. "Oh, go
ahead and smoke."

Opening a drawer in his desk, he took out a small cigar,
a lighter, and an ashtray. He lit the cigar and turned to blow
the smoke away from her.

"You don't have to do that. My father smoked cigars. I
like the smell."

"This is a stogie, ten dollars for twenty. You're forbear-
ing. I've had an unusual day—a rather difficult day, and
I've spent the last hour sitting here and staring at that man
on the cross. At our Lord, trying to understand why he
died."

Sister Brody swallowed the words that came to mind
and remained silent.

"I thought you'd pick me up on that," he said, smiling. "I
don't think I've sinned. I'm not confessing."

"Heaven forbid," she could not help saying.

"Amen. I'm cursed with curiosity, and this morning, before I heard the news of Richard Castle's murder, I had Joe
Hunt come by. You know him, he helped serve last night,
he's Abel Hunt's son. He's at Harvard, a very bright boy,
and what they call a computer nerd. I asked him, in all confidence, to sit down at our computer and find out what he
could about Richard Castle." Donovan paused and shook
the ashes off the cigar.

"What did he find out?" Sister Brody could not help asking.

"Too much. This Internet is a strange and disturbing
place. I found out that it happened when Castle was an Assistant Secretary for Latin American Affairs. The nuns and

lay workers who were raped and killed, the six Jesuit priests who were murdered in cold blood, Archbishop Romero—all of it carried out by murder squads we trained and armed—Castle was one of the men who planned it and pushed it through."

Sister Brody said nothing.

"You don't appear surprised."

"Castle? Yes, that surprises me. I don't think Sally knows anything about that. Castle is dead. Remember, I was there. I saw the bodies. That was many years ago. Is that why you canceled the homily?"

"No, no. I canceled the homily because I can't write one. It goes deeper. Where was I then? Where was the church? Why was this monstrosity buried by the media? Why was the Vatican responding in whispers? Where was the rage?"

"Rage, Father? Is rage a part of our church?"

He dropped the cigar into the ashtray and stared at her.

"Why are Jesuits or nuns or a bishop any different? Over seventy thousand people were murdered in that forsaken little country—and they were all human beings. Isn't that more awful than a handful of priests?"

He spread his arms. "My dear lady, you're right. I am not going to argue with you. You asked me a question, and I am trying to answer it—not for you but for myself. Six million Jews were put to death in the heart of civilized, Catholic Europe. How could that have happened? Why did we let it happen? Don't tell me answers that I already know. It's in the past. There must be forgiveness. But forgiveness is not forgetfulness. The walls of the Vatican, the walls of every church in the world, should have exploded with protest, but where—where was the silence broken?"

"You shouldn't ask me questions like that," Sister Brody said meekly.

"Then who should I ask?"

"Yourself."

He leaned back and clasped his hands. "Thank God, Pat, that I have someone like you."

"Why? To remind you that people are human, weak, often mindless. May I speak freely?"

"Have you ever spoken any other way?" he asked, smiling now.

"Forgive me, Father, you have been too long in Greenwich. Here, things are clean and very nice. Good and evil are cloaked. There are other places all over the earth where good and evil are naked, and evil is very ugly, and death is often beyond any human explanation. I am not berating you. God forbid that I should berate a good man. I have no explanation for what happened in El Salvador or in the Holocaust or in the Catholic Church, for that matter. I have nothing to offer except my faith."

"And you feel that I have lost mine?" the monsignor asked, a note of despair in his voice.

She shook her head. "I would not dare to think that. But even saints have lost their faith."

Then both of them, the man and the woman, retreated into silence. Sister Brody made no move to go, and the monsignor made no move to dismiss her. They both took refuge within themselves. The monsignor was recollecting a time when he was very young, when he believed many, many things that were filled with hope. Sister Brody was wondering how she could help this man in his suffering. She understood what that kind of suffering was like.

Finally, she asked, "May I be even more intrusive than I have been?"

This brought an anguished smile from the priest.

"You are asking how I could be more intrusive," she said.

"No, Pat. Go ahead."

"What do you find when you meditate?"

"It's not what I find, Pat, but what I seek."

"And what do you seek, Father?"

"God."

She nodded.

The monsignor passed a hand over the pile of papers on

his desk. "In there, today, I found the manuscript that Harold Sellig had sent to Herb Greene. Why his wife sent it on to me, I don't know. Sellig has a thorough distaste for clerics of every kind, ministers, priests, rabbis—he excludes no one of the cloth. He was stationed on an aircraft carrier for two years during the Vietnam War, as a naval historian, and he spent time onshore, in part during the Tet offensive. He began the book then . . ." The monsignor's voice trailed away.

"It appears to have had a deep effect on you." This was more a question than an answer.

"It fractured my sense of judgment."

"Why should we have to judge? That's for God, isn't it?"

"Yes, that's for God."

"And we can pray for all three of them, can't we, Father? For the innocent woman, for the good doctor, and for the man who espoused murder. Let Father Garibaldi give the homily. All you have to say is a simple prayer."

"Yes, sister." He had tears in his eyes.

"And now, it's past midnight. We both need our sleep."

"More than you know," the monsignor said. "What would I have done if Castle still lived?"

"My mother used to say, If ifs and ands were pots and pans, how would the tinkers laugh!"

"Yes, of course," he replied, thinking that he would sit up half the night, thinking of a prayer.

"No," Sister Brody said, "with all apology, I think you miss the point. We believe that death is something more than death, but in every case there is a certain terrible sameness. We have surrendered God's greatest gift, the gift of life. Forgive me for reading you a homily. I have no right to, but so long as there is war and starvation and murder and grief beyond measure, we are all assassins, the good and the bad, the meek and the proud. There is the sin that we all share—the sin of indifference."

She had noted that it was past midnight, but Donovan

did not want her to go. He stared at this small, pudgy woman and tried desperately to unravel his own complex inner being; and finally, he said, "The Buddhists write, Do no harm to any sentient being."

"We take it a little further—Love thy brother as thyself."

"Even Castle." He nodded.

"Even Castle."

Sister Brody rose, walked around the desk, and kissed him lightly on his cheek. "Good night, Father. Sleep well." Then she left.

The monsignor sat at his desk for almost an hour after she had gone. He pondered over his work, his life, its barren disappointments, its moments of exultation, its emptiness, and its fullness, and he searched for a link he could break and thereby make himself free. He wandered through a desert called the world we live in, and he recalled the endless parade of faces that had come and gone, and at long last, his mind was still. He picked up his pen and began to write on the pad that lay on his desk:

> *The selfsame moment I could pray;*
> *And from my neck so free*
> *The Albatross fell off, and sank*
> *Like lead into the sea.*